Return to
Harken House

BOOKS BY *Joan Aiken*

Blackground
If I Were You
Mansfield Revisited
Foul Matter
The Girl from Paris
The Weeping Ash
The Smile of the Stranger
Castle Barebane
The Five-Minute Marriage

Last Movement
The Silence of Herondale
Voices in an Empty House
A Cluster of Separate Sparks
The Embroidered Sunset
The Crystal Crow
Dark Interval
Beware of the Bouquet
The Fortune Hunters

JUVENILES

Give Yourself a Fright
A Touch of Chill
The Shadow Guests
Midnight Is a Place
A Whisper in the Night
*The Wolves of Willoughby
    Chase*
Black Hearts in Battersea
Nightbirds on Nantucket
The Cuckoo Tree
The Stolen Lake
Dido and Pa
The Skin Spinners: Poems
*The Green Flash and Other
    Tales*
*The Far Forests: Tales of
    Romance, Fantasy and
    Suspense*
*The Angel Inn by the
    Comtesse de Segur,*
    translated by *Joan Aiken*

Bridle the Wind
Go Saddle the Sea
The Teeth of the Gale
The Faithless Lollybird
Not What You Expected
Arabel's Raven
Arabel and Mortimer
*The Mooncusser's Daughter:
    A Play for Children*
*Winterthing: A Children's
    Play*
Street: A Play for Children
Died on a Rainy Sunday
Night Fall
*Smoke from Cromwell's
    Time and Other Stories*
The Whispering Mountain
A Necklace of Raindrops
*Armitage, Armitage Fly
    Away Home*
The Moon's Revenge

Return to Harken House

Joan Aiken

Delacorte Press

Published by
Delacorte Press
Bantam Doubleday Dell Publishing Group, Inc.
666 Fifth Avenue
New York, New York 10103

This work was first published in Great Britain by
Scholastic Publications Ltd. under the title VOICES.

Library of Congress Cataloging in Publication Data

Aiken, Joan
  [Voices]
  Return to Harken House / Joan Aiken.
     p.   cm.
  Previously published as: Voices. c1988.
  Summary: In the 1930's eleven-year-old Julia goes to spend the
summer with her playwright father and finds that he has abandoned
her to the care of her preoccupied stepmother who seems unaware of
the strange voices that haunt Julia every night.
  ISBN 0-385-29975-3
  [1. Ghosts—Fiction.   2. England—Fiction.]   I. Title.
PZ7.A2695Re   1990
[Fic]—dc20   89-23483
                                                           CIP
                                                            AC

Manufactured in the United States of America

February 1990

10 9 8 7 6 5 4 3 2 1

BVG

Return to
Harken House

Chapter One

THE SHABBY LEATHER SUITCASE, with enough clothes in it for three months, bumped against my shins at each step as I lugged it up the steep cobbled hill.

For five minutes I had waited at the bus stop, until it became dismally plain that nobody had come to meet me; then, puzzled and uneasy, I set off on the short walk to my father's house. Harken House, it was called. I had been born in it, but left it at age four, when my parents were divorced and my mother was given custody of me and Anna and Joe, my elder sister and brother. In the past seven years I had been back here perhaps half a dozen times for short visits.

The weather was close and sultry, for the month of May. And my case was a dead weight, packed by my mother with fanatic care and neatness. "I suppose That Woman will be unpacking for you. . . ." Everything that I could possibly need had been fitted in, a tuppenny red account book to keep record of the ten-shillings spending money she had given me—"Though I daresay Gerald will be providing all sorts of treats"—winter vests, in case the summer turned cold, even a packet of Kotex, though, please heaven, I wouldn't need those for a year or so. "But you never know," said my mother darkly, "what effect such a complete change may produce. Mind you make your bed *properly,* every day, *after* breakfast, and help with the dishes—"

All these warnings made me impatient. "Yes, yes," I had mumbled, not perceiving that what she felt was a need to ward off potential criticism of how she had trained and brought me up.

There were very few cars in the streets; and none on the cobbled ones. All this happened over fifty years ago, way back in the 1930s.

Was Mamm sad at my going away from home? I hadn't stopped to ask myself such a question. Her parting hug had been very long and tight. But at the moment of parting, climbing onto the bus, my whole mind had been thrown forward toward the new experience, the five-hour journey, the start of school, the return to Harken House, the prospect of a whole summer with Gerald. To me, my playwright father was a figure of great romance and glamour. He sent me funny letters (not often). I had seen his name in *print.* There were books by him on the shelf upstairs, by the attic door. The thought of three whole months with him was amazing.

But now, all of a sudden, I felt a complete slump of spirit. *Why* had nobody met me at the bus stop? Hauling the hateful heavy case I was swamped by a great wash of longing for Mamm, for her calm brisk reliability and comfort. "Do try to write every week: I've put in twelve stamped, addressed envelopes." I would have liked to post a letter now, at once, saying *Please can I come home, I don't want to spend a summer in Dune.* But perhaps, after all, Mamm was relieved to be rid of me? Perhaps she was glad of a chance to be on her own with my stepfather and small half-brother? It had given me a dreadful pang when once, helping her make beds, I had remarked probingly, "It's funny that Anna's room is also called the guest room, isn't it?" and Mamm had answered, "Well, she and Joe *are* only guests here, now they're away at college most of the time."

That pang had been so deep and so painful that I hadn't dared say any more, in case my own right to be part of the newly formed family had been called into question.

For the twelfth time I shifted the leather case from one hand to the other. Large, penny-sized drops of rain were now splatting down on the pavement. From the murky sky over the marshes came a low growl of thunder.

My raincoat was tidily folded inside the case. To get it out I'd have to stop, open the case, spoil her careful packing—

"Having trouble, duck?" said a man, overtaking

me. "Got far to go? Looks like a heavy bag for a nipper like you—"

"To Harken House," I said gratefully as he took it from me. "About halfway up the hill."

"Harken House? That's haunted, innit? You going to stay there?"

"My father lives in it," I told him with pride.

"Does he, though? Wouldn't catch me hanging up me hat in there, not for all the herring in Holland. Supposed to be haunted by that old astrologist, innit? You ever see him?"

"No," I was obliged to admit. I didn't tell him how seldom I had been in the house since I left at age four. "But my father has—or heard things—"

"He really? I never! He must be a cool one!"

"He's a writer."

"Oh, well, that accounts, dunnit? He can use all that kind of weird stuff for his writing, can't he? There you are, then, love, ta-ra," and, glancing up at the stone slab over the door that said JOSHUA HARKIN 1641–1693, he sketched a friendly salute and strode on up the hill.

Suppose the door is locked? I thought, with a cold twist of real fright. What do I do then? But the brass doorknob turned easily, and I walked into the hall. (Nobody locked doors in those days.) The smell of the house greeted me like a womb, a bird's nest, instantly remembered from early childhood—old dry dark wood, damp stone, gently leaking gas, closeness, secrecy. Bats, musty bird's feathers or droppings, dry rot, dust. The front hall was just as I remembered: L shaped, very high, a door leading through to the dining room and kitchen, a stair (uncarpeted black wood with square black newel post) leading up to the next floor.

"Er—hullo?" I called timidly. My voice seemed no more than a thread in the big hollow space. Nobody answered.

After a moment or two I started up the stairs, leaving my bag below standing on the thin Turkish rug. And just at the corner I came face to face with my stepmother, "That Woman," as Mamm called her, Trudl, as she was known to everybody else. She was Austrian, small, blond, animated, and spoke English far more clearly and correctly than most people born in the country. Her gilt hair was twined round her head in a coronet. She wore a white blouse and a dirndl skirt. When she saw me her mouth dropped open in total surprise.

"*Julia!* But—are you expected—?"

Quite evidently I was *not* expected.

"I—I thought Ma—my mother wrote to Gerald?" I said unhappily.

"Gerald is not here. *Dinner at Delphi* is to be acted at Lucerne and he has gone there for the rehearsals and to help with the text. . . . But come up, come up, of course. It is very nice that you are here," she added hastily.

"I—my school starts on Monday—"

Her hand flew to her mouth. She stared at me over it.

"Your *school*! Of course it does! What a very very lucky thing that you came today. That will give you— let's see—tomorrow to get settled. Now wait, wait, and I will quickly put some sheets on a bed—"

Lucky? I thought confusedly, this was how the

whole arrangement was planned, ever so long ago. But it was clear that, for one reason or another, Trudl had completely forgotten about it.

"Here," she said, handing me a pair of sheets. "You take these, I follow with blankets. It will be quite nice for me, having you, it will be company, indeed." And she led the way up another steep black stair, much narrower, this one; then through a tiny room where, I dimly remembered, Mamm used to have her sewing machine, then down four steps, across a big double room with a studio window—

"Anna and I always used to sleep in the room that looks out on the garden—" I suggested hopefully. That was a snug little room which had the sun for most of the day.

"So? But just now I am using that for a study. Very fast, just now, I translate others of your father's plays into German, in case somebody else wishes to use one. Anyway, along here you will be nice and private— you and I need not disturb each other. You may read all night if you wish!"

We had ended up in a room beyond the study—a long narrow room, facing north, lit by nothing but a small skylight in its sloping ceiling. It was rather dark, and the floor, ancient black timbers, also sloped slightly uphill.

With a nod, Trudl dropped her bundle of blankets on the bed.

"Come down when you have your bed made, and we will then think about supper. Can you eat sausages, I wonder?"

Her voice was clear and brisk, like a woodpecker tapping on a tree. She clicked away in her little high-heeled sandals and I set myself to the job of making the bed, rather messily and lumpily. But nobody was going to notice or criticize. The room where she had installed me was well away from the main part of the house; in fact it lay above the next-door building, which was one enormous two-story room, now converted into an art gallery. There was certainly no doubt of my privacy. The art gallery, I knew, was closed at night. My father's big double study stood empty, his desk unnaturally tidy, the books, instead of lying around in heaps, all neatly arranged on the shelves round the walls. Through the huge window, with its single pane of glass, one could see all the way across the marshes to a faint silver line along the horizon, which was the sea.

Beyond the study was the sewing room, up four steps, beyond *that* the steep stairs leading down to the bathroom on the floor below. . . . Should I ever be able to muster up courage to go all that way in the dark, I wondered, supposing I had to get up and pee in the night?

"Here is your bag," said Trudl, returning with it. "Now, see, there is a hook on the back of the door, and I daresay these drawers are empty." She pulled one out. It came with a grinding rattle and she added, "Oh, yes, and now I remember, Gerald did, of course, know that you were coming. Only I had forgotten that it was quite so *soon*. But I believe he left a note for you—yes, here it is—and some books—"

At this, my spirits, which were very low, perked up a little. Perhaps he would say when he was coming back—

"Now I am going to run down the road to the

butcher," said Trudl, "and buy a pound of sausages. When I am alone I just have fruit. There will just be time before he closes. . . . So, take as long as you please with your unpacking."

I heard her tip-tap away again down the uncarpeted stairs as I fully opened the stiff top drawer in the gray-painted deal chest, which, like the kitchen chair, the thin mat, and the cot bed, was the very plainest that money could buy. My father only *just* scraped a living from his plays.

Dear Jukes, he had written, *too bad I can't be there to see you enrolled with the Norns. The old girls look as if eye of newt and toe of frog would be on their daily timetable, but I daresay they are really mild as milk. You will probably soon have them eating out of your hand. I hope school proves to be fun—though I never thought much of it myself. . . .*

Here's a few books you may like to read. Perhaps you'd like to try your hand at playwriting?

This Lucerne foray could make all our fortunes yet. Let's hope so. I have to be there to make sure they don't mangle the text. Is there a chance you'll still be in Dune when I come a-flitting back, I wonder? Don't know yet when that will be. Love, Nuncle.

For some reason *Nuncle* was what my father liked us to call him, but I found it a bit embarrassing and preferred to use his Christian name.

The note, like all his letters, was typed, obviously at high speed, for it was full of mistakes, and signed with a hasty pencil flourish.

When I looked at the books—a small bundle of faded volumes—I felt let down and cheated. They were *plays*—peering at the tarnished gilt lettering on the faded spines I read unfamiliar names—Marston, Webster, Marlowe. And there was Shakespeare's *Henry IV,* parts I and II.

Why in the world should Gerald think I would want to read *those*? I wondered crossly. I'm only eleven, can he have forgotten that? Perhaps he's confusing me with Anna?

I peered again at the fusty old plays, which seemed to be full of doom and dread and horrible goings-on, maniacs laughing and heroines being strangled. A rickety kitchen table stood at the end of the room, under the skylight. I stacked the books on it, and put beside them Mamm's little alarm clock, which she had lent me. "Because you may need to wake yourself in the morning, for school," she had said, obviously not trusting That Woman to do so. "But you will take care of it, won't you?"

Quite a few tears fell on to my neatly folded clothes as I laid them in the unfriendly drawers, each of which jibbed and stuck as I tried to drag it open. I felt desperately cast away and forlorn. Around this time, at home, I would have been laying the table for supper, Mamm would be at her cookery, chopping and clinking in the kitchen, my stepfather would be energetically rattling away on the piano, while my little half-brother, in his cot upstairs, would be far from asleep, quite the reverse, singing loudly, along with the piano music but out of tune, so that his voice echoed down the stairs. The whole house would be alive with cheerful activity. Whereas here . . .

There was not a single sound to be heard in the house, save my own furtive sobs.

I drew a shaky breath and listened. Dune was a

very quiet town, because of the cobbled streets. They were too narrow, steep, and bumpy for motor traffic, which mostly used a ring road outside the old town wall. After six, once the shops in the High Street had closed, there was hardly any noise at all, not even voices or footsteps. All I could hear was the keening of swallows and swifts round the old red chimney pots. Where did people go? Home, I supposed, to eat their evening meal and listen to the radio. (For this was in the thirties, remember, before the days of television).

I strained to listen even harder. Always, at home —(this old, cold vacuum of a house, although my birthplace, was not my home, I swore, no, never, never)—at home there were always country sounds to be heard, the hens next door, cows mooing on their way to be milked, the rasp of a saw, dogs barking, the clank of a bucket in a well, the creak of a handle. Here: nothing, except my own hiccuping breath.

Ashamed of what I knew Mamm would think of me, for being such a crybaby, I put away the last neat pile of undervests and remembered with a spurt of hope that, somewhere about the house, three or four children's books remained, accidentally left behind by Joe and Anna at the time of the split. *White Fang, The Call of the Wild, Hans Brinker*—not my favorites, but a lot easier and more interesting than the plays of Webster and Marlowe. I must ask Trudl if she knew where they had been put. And—yes—Anna had said something about a pile of old sixpenny paperback thrillers, bought by my elders when they were younger, kept always hidden away under a loose floorboard, because Gerald would never have countenanced their spending their money on such rubbish.

"Do have a look and see if they are still there,"
Anna had said, laughing, when she heard I was to
spend the whole summer at school in Dune. "The
loose board is in Joe's attic, under the bed. Very likely
nobody has ever found them."

Having sniffed my nose clear and wiped my eyes,
I went cautiously across Gerald's tidy study, up the
four steps, through the empty sewing room, then
climbed the ship's ladder that led to the attics. From
the window of the right-hand one, where Joe had
slept, you could climb out into a gully between two
gables of roof. (I had been too small in those days, but
Anna and Joe had done it.) Then you could climb all
the way, along the ancient red-tiled roofs, to the end
of the street. And there was a great view, over the
steeply down-dropping houses, across the marsh to
the sea two miles away.

Rain was still drumming down on the tiles that
sloped to a peak directly over my head. This was
certainly not a day for roof exploration. The thunder
had never come close, but it was still there, muttering
quietly in the distance.

But the loose board . . .

Kneeling on the square of rush mat by the bed
(another iron army cot) I felt about underneath it.
The boards were furred with dust; plainly no one
cleaned up here very often. ("I wonder if That
Woman cleans her own house?" Mamm had remarked meditatively. "Or can they afford to have
someone come in?" My mother did all her own house-
work, as well as teaching me my lessons.)

Yes! One of the boards shifted when I pressed it.
And when I pushed down hard at one end, and

hoisted the other, scrabbling with my fingernails, a two-foot section tilted, to reveal a cobwebby cavity underneath. I had to move the cot aside before I could get the board right out. Then, looking in, I discovered Joe and Anna's secret hoard—four yellow-jacketed novels by Edgar Wallace, *The Four Just Men, The Sinister Man, The Angel of Terror, The Book of All Power,* with lurid pictures on the covers; also two others, *The Lair of the White Worm* and *Dracula* by a writer I had never heard of, Bram Stoker.

In triumph I surveyed my trove. I felt like a tracker in the wilderness finding a cache of provisions, chocolate, fruitcake, pemmican (whatever that was). I had never been able to make any headway with the literary works on Gerald's shelves. But these books (they looked madly exciting) should last me for several weeks. And by that time I would have found other sources of reading matter. Schools had libraries, didn't they?

Greatly cheered, I put all but one of the books back into the hole (where there was also a Rowntree's plain chocolate wrapper, slightly nibbled at the edges) left *The Lair of the White Worm* in my bedroom, and washed my dusty hands in the bathroom, which was on the floor below. This was exactly as I remembered it, high, dark and narrow, with a huge tarnished brass geyser, taller than I was, perched over the bath, and a smell that tickled my chest and made me cough, of escaping gas, toothpaste, and damp.

Then I ran down the last flight of stairs to the ground floor and through the dining room to the kitchen, where Trudl was frying sausages. Her shiny, scrubbed-looking face was pink and flushed—with hard work? with annoyance?—but the smile she gave me was friendly enough.

"Just in time to lay the table! Do you like mustard? If you do, you can mix some."

"I don't like mustard, thank you."

"Then we need not bother. Gerald always wished for it. And he makes a great fuss—it has to be just so, not too thick, not too thin. But tell me"—as she carried the plates to the table—"whose idea was it, that you come here to school? For you go on to a big boarding-school in the autumn, isn't that so? Where you will remain for several years? Why, then, come here to Dune, just for the one term?"

Rather blankly I said that I thought it had been Gerald's idea. He had written to Mamm, I believed, suggesting it. (I would dearly have loved to see that letter, but was never given a chance to do so.) "Gerald thinks it might be easier for you to start at boarding school if you had been to a day school at least for a little while first," Mamm had said to me in March. "What do you think?"

The prospect of boarding school in the autumn had been looming already, for the last eighteen months, like a monsoon cloud. My sister Anna had always cried for two days at least before the start of every term. Now the threat for me had been moved forward by five months.

I muttered, "Perhaps. . . ."

"Gerald says there is a nice little school just round the corner from Harken House. Sunnyhay, it's called. Run by three old ladies, sisters–"

The Norns, I remembered Gerald had called

them in his note: *Too bad I can't be there to see you enrolled with the Norns.*

Furiously I thought, he didn't *bother* to be here. He just didn't bother. He could have been here, if he'd really wanted to.

Echoing my thought, Trudl said, "Gerald makes these good plans, but then he forgets about them. Poor Julia! I suppose you were very happy at the thought of spending the summer with him."

"Won't he come back from Lucerne when the play is finished?"

She looked vague and doubtful. "It is not certain. . . ." Quite plainly, she did not intend to talk about Gerald's plans. "But never mind," she went on at once, "you and I can have a nice summer together. While you are busy with your schoolwork, I must be translating his other plays, I must work hard too—in hopes the Lucerne company will put them on—but in the evenings we can go to the beach, or for picnics. We will have fun, I promise. Pfui to Gerald!" She snapped her fingers, laughed, and lit a cigarette.

"Trudl, who were the Norns?"

She looked perplexed for a moment, then her brow cleared. "Ah, I remember, it was what Gerald called those old ladies at your school. The Norns— they are the three sisters who look after Odin's ash tree. Urd, Skuld and, now, who is the third one? Ah, I have it, she is Verdandi. They are the past, present, and future, you know. They sit under the tree, weaving their web of fate and guarding the three golden apples. Three nice old ladies! So! Let us hope they teach you well. And now I think you should go to bed —you look tired and pale and have had a long day.

You can read in bed—I checked that there is a bulb in your bedside lamp."

"Shouldn't I help with the washing up?" I asked dutifully, mindful of Mamm's warnings.

Trudl shrugged. "Two plates? What a great labor! No, you are very well trained, I can see, but that is not necessary. You may wash the lunch things tomorrow if you wish. Then, on Monday, Mrs. Butcher comes and puts us all to rights."

So that answered one of Mamm's questions.

I went slowly up the steep stairs—Trudl was right, I did feel extremely tired; paused at bathroom level for a fast and skimpy wash and tooth-brushing, then toiled on up the next, steeper flight.

Nightgowned and ready for bed, I decided that *The Lair of the White Worm* looked too frightening for just now, and remembered that I had meant to ask Trudl about those three or four children's books left behind by my elders. Well, Trudl surely would not scold me if I went downstairs again—she had not given the impression of a fierce disciplinarian.

Barefoot, I pattered down the two flights, through the dining room, and into the kitchen. The supper things had been put away, rather sketchily—the bread and butter and a jug of milk were still on the kitchen table—*"Slipshod,"* I could hear Mamm say with compressed lips—but Trudl herself was nowhere to be seen.

"Trudl?" I called, but received no answer. Could she be out in the garden? Surely not. The relentless rain still splashed down.

Failing to find her on the ground floor, I retreated

upstairs, but she was not in the bathroom or first-floor sitting-room.

"Trudl! Where are you?"

She was not in her bedroom, on the next floor; nor in the room I had once shared with Anna, now a workroom, where another kitchen table was covered with sheets of paper and reference books. But luckily, in a corner bookshelf here, I found *White Fang* and the other books. Feeling a little more secure in the possession of these, I went back to bed and opened *White Fang.* But where could Trudl have gone? Out, in this weather, to buy cigarettes? Or to see a friend? I wondered how long it would be before she came back, and if I would be able to hear the front door when she did. It seemed unlikely—there were two stories and three rooms in between.

It wasn't quite dark yet—dusk, only; but soon it would be too dark to read. I switched on my bedside light, and was half sorry I had done so, because it made the dimness beyond the light seem like full darkness.

"Dark spruce forest frowned on either side the frozen waterway," I read unhappily. Then I read it again. Then I closed the book.

White Fang begins gloomily with a lot of dark and cold and hardship—savage sled dogs continually fight each other and are beaten by their Indian masters. It is not until the very end of the story that White Fang finds himself a loving home. Suddenly I knew with certainty that I wasn't in the mood for all that fierceness and suffering.

Inside me, like a tidal wave, I could feel another attack of tears piling up, drawing back, arching higher and higher; to distract myself from that, I thought about my feet, which were extremely cold; I could tell that the one thin blanket was not going to be sufficient. I took down my raincoat from the hook on the back of the door and spread that over the bed. It didn't make very much difference. Then, because I was out of bed anyway, I thought I had better go down to the bathroom again. Perhaps by now Trudl would have come back.

There was no sign or sound of her anywhere downstairs. I felt nervous about pulling the lavatory chain, it had seemed to make such a colossal noise in the empty, echoing house. Before doing so, I poked about in the bathroom for a while, sniffing the cake of pink soap, undoing the cap of Trudl's toothpaste to try what it tasted like. In the bath tray there lay a loofah. I had never seen such a thing before and prodded it with my finger, wondering how it was used.

Then I heard a tiny, queer hiss, like the buzz of a wasp in a jam jar, or a bluebottle caught in a spiderweb. So faint was the sound that I *could* have imagined it; but I knew I had not. With a nervous gasp, I pulled the chain, drowning any other sound in the loud gush of released waters. Then I raced up the steep black stairs, through the sewing room, across the wide study, now completely dark, to the welcome square of light framed by my bedroom doorway, and hurled myself, quivering, into bed.

I shan't be able to *stand* it here, I thought.

Next minute, I was asleep.

Chapter Two

NEXT MORNING, the house felt more cheerful. My own room was rather somber, because the one skylight window faced northward, but sunshine came slantways through the big studio window next door, the sea shone like a flashing sword across the horizon, and I could smell a faint welcome whiff of coffee and food. Trudl's voice called up the stair to tell me that she was through in the bathroom. Brushing my teeth I sneered at myself for last night's childish fright; what could I have thought I heard, for heaven's sake?

"Have you ever seen a ghost in this house, Trudl?" I asked at breakfast, half joking, but half remembering the man who had carried my bag.

She answered with gravity, "Julia, if you had seen and heard some of the terrible things I have, that are going on in Europe now, you would not bother your head about imaginary fears such as ghosts"—and she told me a bit about Adolf Hitler, how she had managed to get out of Austria, with Gerald's help, and had come to England, where she was safe, but many of her friends and family were left behind, still in danger. The fact that Gerald had helped her made me feel more friendly toward him, and I resolved to try and read the plays he had left out for me. Not today— but sometime.

After I had helped with the breakfast dishes and made my bed—Trudl asked if I had been warm enough and I answered truthfully that I had not, so she found me another blanket—I said I would take a walk round the town. Good idea, said Trudl; I would see that they were building a new boat basin down in the river—local rumors said it was a submarine basin but that must be nonsense, for there wouldn't be room. A submarine could never make its way up the winding muddy Dune River.

Trudl was going to work on her translation. See you at lunchtime, she said, and went off with a no-nonsense air to her workroom.

I had never felt so idle and free before.

Of course the very first thing I did was to run round the corner into Chapel Passage so as to take a survey of the school where I would be starting on Monday.

The school in fact occupied the chapel of Chapel Passage—a little flint building left empty and unwanted when a religious group called the Gideon

Free Methodists died out for lack of new members, Trudl had told me. The windows were narrow and set high in the walls; even on tiptoe I could not reach to see in. The building stood sideways on to the lane, fronting on its own little yard, which was enclosed by a high wall and a high wooden gate; I peered through a crack but could see little beyond a flagged pavement and a tub of blue hydrangeas.

Not wishing to be caught spying about, I wandered on through the town, which was tidy and silent for Sunday. (There were many fewer tourists in those days.)

Up and down the seven cobbled streets I ambled, gazing into the windows of closed shops, slipping down narrow alleyways which ended in stone-walled lookout points where bowmen had once watched for the French. I went down a flight of steps into the sunny, grassy Gun Gardens, where some ancient cannon pointed their muzzles vaguely toward France, and then down a longer, steeper flight to the bottom of the cliff which defended Dune on three sides. I walked diagonally across the green playing fields called the Town Salts, and along to the shaggy piece of land known as the Shipyard, where great old logs lay about, weathering, and huge ancient pairs of iron wheels, gun carriages left over from World War I, stood half smothered in grass and weeds. Beyond them lay the towpath and the gray-brown tidal river; tide was half out, and when I threw a stone it fell with a wonderful splot! and sank out of sight into the deep mudbank.

Suppose a person fell in there? I wondered. How deep down would they sink?

I saw a dead gull which lay half sunk, its poor feathers ruffled and muddy; that reminded me uneasily of a moment in last night's procession of troubled dreams. A large white bird, perhaps an eagle, had perched near me and had not flown away even when I moved closer to it; that was because it was sick, I realized, and wondered anxiously if it would die, if I ought to help it, do something about it—but would it let me?

While I stood wondering the bird blinked open its nearest eye, which had been shut, and said in a hoarse, harsh human voice: *"Listen!"*

That was all; no more.

After lunch, Trudl carried out her promise to take me to the beach, but the trip was not a great success. The walk there was long, and very dull, out of the town along a main road past new little square red-brick houses, then by a track across the flat marsh, through sheep-cropped fields and over nine or ten footbridges that spanned wide tidal ditches. The last bit was the worst: a long trudge over a mile of shingly desert where nothing grew but gorse and sea thistles. The sea was invisible all this time behind a row of sand dunes, and when we finally slogged through a dry sandy gap between these, the sea still seemed a huge distance away, for the tide was full out across wide, flat sands. The sky had clouded and misted, a small chill wind blew, so there was no temptation to explore farther along the beach; anyway we had walked, I thought, quite far enough already. Trudl seemed to be of the same mind. "Well—now you know your way," she said in a voice of relief. "You can come and swim whenever you want. *Can* you swim, by the way?"

"Sort of," I said.

"Perhaps they will have outings from your school. Or you can come with friends. You are sure to make friends"—on a note of hope. "Now, I think we had better go back—unless you wish to stay and play on the beach? But I must be getting on with my work."

I disclaimed the least wish to play on the beach, and we started on the long walk home. I fell farther and farther behind as she strode quickly and impatiently over the shingle and the thistly pastures, on short stocky legs with strong muscular calves. By the time I reached Harken House she was already up in her workroom, typing away.

It was plain that afternoon tea played no part in Trudl's regime, so after roaming aimlessly about the house for a while, I settled in Gerald's study, where there was a hard narrow chaise longue beside the big studio window, and began to read *The Lair of the White Worm.*

The picture on the jacket showed a huge white serpent with green flashing eyes, rearing up out of a forest at night. The beams from its eyes, like lighthouse rays, traveled right across the surrounding countryside. The story took rather a long time to get started, but was terrifying when it did, about an evil lady who changed into a snake at night—a were-snake. In the end she was caught and killed. As soon as that happened she turned into an enormous mass of putrefying jelly and horridness that seethed and heaved in a cleft in the ground before at last it settled down and turned to ordinary mud. Like the tidal riverbanks, I thought, and imagined them as great wriggly serpents, following the course of the river. I read and read, with my eyes starting out of my head, and went downstairs rather sick and dazed when finally roused by Trudl's voice calling me to supper.

During the meal I wanted to ask her more about Joshua Harkin, why people believed that he haunted the house; but instead she talked about German troops marching, three months ago, into Austria; and about something called the *Anschluss*, which I didn't fully understand. "It is all Nazis now in Austria," she said. "I came to England in time, but my brother and friends are still there, writing against Hitler and the Nazis; I am afraid for them."

I went up to bed with a vague picture in my head of a black snaky tide creeping across the map of Europe. "He will not stop at Austria," Trudl said. "He says the Germans need more *Lebensraum*. That means living space, room to live in. Next he will take Czechoslovakia. He is already saying that many who live in that country are really Germans."

That night again I had bad dreams.

ON MONDAY MORNING Mrs. Butcher told me that Trudl had gone out for the day. "Up to London, yer ma's gone—"

"Stepmother—" I corrected her automatically.

"Caught the ten to eight, said she'd be back suppertime. (On the 'alf six, likely.) I'll leave a cold pie, though, so's you don't 'ave to worry. Ask me, you could do with a bit of feeding up—skinny little tuppence-haporth, aren't you?" she said, plunking a boiled egg in front of me.

Mrs. Butcher had a wrinkled, highly colored face, two bright little eyes, and a nose on whose sharp tip a drip hung; her head was tied in a scarf and she herself wrapped in a navy floral print overall, over a brown serge skirt, black stockings, and worn black sandshoes. I didn't dare say that I loathed boiled eggs, for they seemed to be the standard breakfast here. Trudl had given me one yesterday. A larger problem dragged at my mind.

"But I'm supposed to start school today—"

"Oo's stopping yer? Know where it is, don't yer? Want me to go round with ye?" said Mrs. Butcher with fearful scorn. "You wouldn't want *that*, I shouldn't think."

No, no, I said hastily, I would take myself round. Er—what time did school begin?

Half past eight in *her* young days, Mrs. Butcher replied tartly. "Run upstairs now and get yer things together—and brush yer hair a bit tidier—looks like you bin dragged through a holly hedge."

I felt a guilty pang toward Mamm, who had carefully washed my hair just before I left home, and had meticulously ironed the school uniform dresses, white cotton smothered with purple polka dots. (The purple uniform blazer, which I admired, in the catalogue, she had thought a needless extravagance, just for one term. "Wear your gray cardigan. . . .")

Thus dressed, carrying a music case with pencils and notebook, I walked down steep Harbor Hill, and up into Chapel Passage. I felt sick.

Mrs. Butcher, softening a little just before I left, had said, "I'll be here when you gets back, duck, to give you your bit of dinner." And she muttered something about flibbertigibbets under her breath, then added, "And don't you let them old tabbies put you down. Your Dad's as good as them, if your stepma is a foreigner."

I had just reached the school gate when, luckily for me, a mother-with-child arrived from the opposite direction, so we all went in together.

There seemed to be about twenty-five people thronged in the little building (which smelled of kerosene lamps and furniture polish). A deafening clatter of voices rebounded from all the polished surfaces—lino floor, little cork-topped desks, plaster walls, map, blackboard, wooden shelves.

I stood paralyzed with shyness until a voice said kindly, "Ah, and this must be Julia. We have been expecting you, my dear."

The mother who had delivered her child now left, and so did another; slowly, the group around me sorted itself out into three old ladies and twenty children.

"We have three classes," said the tallest old lady, who had spoken to me—she was Miss Sybil, the eldest sister, I learned later. "You, Julia dear, form the top class with Timothy Bellyap here. Miss Lucy looks after the eight-to-tens, and Miss Madge has the five-to-sevens." Miss Lucy was the small plump sister, Miss Madge the dry, rangy, slightly mad-looking one with protruding lower lip.

Three groups sorted themselves out.

"Now, shall we say the Lord's Prayer?" suggested Miss Sybil.

While we did that, I took stock of Timothy Bellyap, the only other person in my class. Then the smaller children sat down with their teachers while Timothy and I were escorted to a tiny annex room where there was *just* enough space for two desks. Hitler wouldn't have been satisfied, I thought. Miss Sybil, who had gold-gray hair swept into a bun, a strong jaw, a sweet smile, and a voice like liquid honey, proceeded to teach us sums and geography. The words she used for things were quite unknown to me—words like *product, quotient, multiplicand*—but the subjects and processes seemed familiar.

Then we had milk and biscuits, then Miss Madge, who had gray hair in a knob on top of her head, taught us history and poetry. Miss Madge, despite her odd looks, was rather a good teacher, I thought; she had a dry way of making remarks, snapping them off sharply like the sound of a nutcracker; when you thought about them afterward they turned out to have been rather funny.

My dread of school began to abate. Miss Sybil and Miss Madge weren't bad. Tim seemed harmless enough. He was a plumpish boy, fresh faced and mouse haired, bigger than me but younger. And the rest of the children were too young to worry about— so what could be the reason for the strong feeling of darkness and trouble at the back of my mind? Was it connected with last night's dreams? I could remember nothing of them save a feeling of furious anger—I had woken once, screaming, *"Stop it! Stop it!"* at the top of my lungs. (Just as well, I thought in the morning, that three rooms, four steps, and a landing lay between my room and Trudl's.)

Why did I find myself, all the time, straining my ears to catch the echo of some tiny sound?

At the lunch break most of the children, who lived in Dune, went home.

Tim, who lived a mile outside the town, pulled out a packet of sandwiches.

I ran down Chapel Passage, turned right up Harbor Hill, and in at the door of Harken House, vaguely hoping that Trudl would have come back—but of course she had not. Mrs. Butcher had a plate of stew waiting for me, and stood sociably resting the palms of her hands on the table while I ate it.

"Tuck in, duck, that's right; got to eat to keep your spirits up in this old house, and that's the truth."

"Why, Mrs. Butcher?"

"Wouldn't catch me living in the hole," she said earnestly, then, recollecting, perhaps, that I might later be spending the evening there by myself, until Trudl returned from London, she changed the subject and talked about my father and Trudl.

" 'E met 'er in Austria and she told 'im she'd never be able to get out, not unless she could marry an Englishman. So your Pa obliged."

My mother's version had been slightly different, and less heroic. "That woman just grabbed him. . . ."

But, for once, I was not interested in family history. I wanted to know about Joshua Harkin.

"*Why* does he haunt the house, Mrs. Butcher? Have *you* ever seen him?"

"Now, that's quite enough of that. Finish your rice pudding and run along back to school."

When I arrived home from school at four, I discovered that Mrs. Butcher had thoughtfully dispatched her daughter Wyn to keep me company.

Wyn was fourteen, thin and pimply, her lank fair hair kept off her pale cheeks by a pair of imitation tortoiseshell barrettes. She had brought two bags of potato chips and suggested we go out into the small garden behind Harken House. This had a tiny cobbled terrace, a small brick-edged flower-bed where London Pride grew and a larger one, outside the kitchen window, full of mint that had grown as high as my waist. The garden was enclosed by a six-foot flint wall.

"Many's the poor man's lost his wife,
Over the garden wall!"

sang Wyn.

"Many's the tomcat's lost his life
Over the garden wall!"

She also sang about the king's horses and the king's men; and that it wasn't going to rain no more, no more.

Rapidly becoming bored with all this singing—Wyn had a whiny scrannel voice like water dripping into a rusty can—I tried asking her about Joshua Harkin. Perhaps she would be more prepared to talk than her mother had been.

But her hand flew to her mouth.

"Oh, I can't tell you that; not *ever;* Mum'd kill me."

"Why?"

"You're just a little kiddy. That ain't for your ears."

"Why not?"

"That's too frightening."

Affronted, I went and fetched some of my books—*Dracula, The Lair of the White Worm,* and a couple of the Edgar Wallace thrillers. "Look, these are the books I read—I bet they are much more frightening than any old ghost story."

"Coo," she said, greedily examining the picture of the white serpent towering above the forest. "What's this one about, then?"

I gave her an outline of the story and she listened with starting eyes.

"And then she all turns to *jelly*? Coo! I'd like to read that bit. Can you find it?"

When I had found her the bit she read it with frowning, labored concentration, breathing heavily, marking each word by moving a sprig of mint along the printed line.

"So now," I said, "you tell me about Joshua Harkin."

"Oh." She thought for a moment. "Well, rightee-oh. Anyway, it's ever such a long time ago. In King Charles's days."

"Which King Charles?"

"Him that had his head cut off. Old Joshua Harkin lived here with his daughter."

"What was her name?"

"Patty. That was short for Patience. And Patience was her nature, poor thing," said Wyn, warming to her story, "for they say he was a stern hard father, kept her at work all the day long, kept finding fault, whipped her if the meals weren't to his liking, never let her have any fun."

"Poor Patty," I said, wondering if it was worse to

have a stern hard father or one who never showed up at all. "So what happened?"

"They say that old Joshua was a philosophist."

"What's that?"

"I dunno," admitted Wyn handsomely. "But he could do ever so many different things—like, he cured folks with his medicines, and prophesied what was going to happen, and looked at the stars through a spyglass; and he was an alley-chemist, not like Mr. Ryder in the High Street, one of that sort who could turn iron into gold."

"Could he *really?*"

"So people said. There was this young fellow, this prentice boy, working for him. Ralph, his name was. Ralph and Patty fell in love—she used to slip out, after dark, and meet him in this very garden. Nothing bad, you know," said Wyn quickly, glancing round at the cobbled paving and the overgrown mint, "just to see each other where old Joshua couldn't be nagging and jawing on at them. Moan, moan, he was at them all the time. Wouldn't let them be friends—said they was to mind their work, not waste time in canoodling; and he told Patty, if she ever did marry, it better be someone with more money than a prentice boy. But Joshua didn't want her to marry, not particular. She was too handy in the house, see, doing the cooking and grinding up his medicine powders."

"What happened?"

"The two o' them run off and got themselves married," Wyn said impressively. "O' course, in those days prentice boys was bound to their masters for a number of years, like it might be five; Ralph could have been sent to prison for running off. So they went over to France—there was lots o' smugglers' boats passing back and forth in them times—and got married in France. But then Ralph fell sick."

"What of?"

"Nobody could tell. Some o' the French, where they was lodging, thought it might be the plague, and asked them to leave. Patty believed her father had put a curse on Ralph; he'd threatened that, you see. So they came back to England, and put up, secretly, with Ralph's auntie, who lived here in Dune, by the Land Gate; and then Patty went to her father and told him she was sorry, and asked him to take the curse off."

"She must have been a brave girl."

"I wouldn't have wanted to see the old misery," agreed Wyn. "But old Joshua was mild as milk, seemingly; said he'd missed them and would forgive them if only they'd come back and work for him again. And he mixed up some medicine and gave it to Patty for Ralph, that he said would cure him."

"Did it cure him?"

"No, it killed him. Leastways, he died. So then there was a lot of talk in the town, and folks said Joshua had killed his son-in-law on purpose, and he was a murderer, and a wicked wizard, and ought to be burned. A lot of them thought that. He wasn't a popular man, see, for he always kept hisself to hisself. So a big crowd went to his house and grabbed him, and took him down on the Town Salts, and piled up a bonfire, and they was a-going to burn him."

"And *did* they?" I asked, my heart quickening. There had been a fire in last night's bad dreams, I remembered; flames blazing to heaven. I had forgotten it up to this moment. There had been something dreadful about that fire—

"No," said Wyn, "there was a big thunderstorm, flashes o' lightning and buckets of rain. The fire wouldn't light, and in the commotion, Joshua escaped and ran back to his house and barred himself in; shouted to them that if they broke in he'd jump off the roof and fly away and escape them that way."

"*Could* he fly?"

I felt a deep envy for Joshua. Flying was a skill I'd always felt unjustly deprived of; I often dreamed of flying, and still felt that it must be possible to learn it.

"People said he'd invented a flying machine. In the end, though, they did get into the house; some wanted to burn it down, but the mayor wouldn't have that, for the houses next door might have burned too. Anyhow, when they got into the house, he wasn't there. Not anywhere. So then lots of them said the devil must have come for him. But then, they said, he left a curse—"

"A curse?"

"Coo!" said Wyn, suddenly breaking off as she heard the church clock strike seven. "I oughta be home. Mum'll murder me. Hatta be at work tomorrow, seven o'clock." Fourteen-year-old Wyn had a job in the mornings, cleaning, for Mrs. Spearpoint, who kept the Pedlar's Pack Gift Shop.

"But Trudl's not come home yet," I said, dismayed.

"Oh, well, likely she'll be along on the ten-thirty. You better put yourself to bed soon's you had your supper. Cuddle up tight under the covers," advised

Wyn, and ran off singing, "There ain't no sense, Sitting on the fence, All by yourself *in* the moonlight."

I ate my cold pie alone in the dining room, starting nervously at every sound. And there were plenty of sounds in Harken House, creaks from old boards, gurgles from the aged plumbing, muffled thumps and rumbles from the prehistoric boiler in the kitchen.

I tried to distract myself by reading *Dracula*, but the details in that book about chests of earth, dripping fangs, and buzzing bluebottle flies were not a happy distraction. When I heard a creak I wondered if it was the lid of a chest full of earth opening. And I could certainly hear the buzzing of flies—quite clear and distinct, like interference on a radio station. Zizz, zizz, zizz. And again, zizz, wizz, wizz.

I fled up to bed, dropping *Dracula* in Gerald's study, taking with me *The Call of the Wild,* which I hoped would be more soothing and comfortable bedtime company. But the trouble about *The Call of the Wild* is that it has a most mournful ending, with kind John Thornton killed by Indians, and the hero dog, Buck, returning every year to howl over his grave; it is a somber tale, and in between, through it and beyond it, I could not help remembering Wyn's tale of Joshua Harkin, and speculating about its details. For it had all taken place in this house. Where, for instance, had Joshua worked? Which room had been his laboratory? Perhaps Gerald's study next door? And what about Ralph the apprentice? How and where did he carry out his duties? What would an alchemist's boy do, anyway, apart from grinding up powders? Perhaps he brewed and distilled? But what did those words mean? And where was Patty, meanwhile, how was she occupied? Cleaning the house, going to market, cooking the meals? Did she pick mint in the garden? Wash clothes in a wooden tub? Her father found fault continually and beat her if the bread failed to rise or the meat was tough—I imagined his harsh, penetrating voice, like a hacksaw blade biting into metal. And she, poor thing, would try to defend herself, protesting that the wood was damp, the yeast poor quality, the fire would not burn up—I could almost hear their opposed voices weaving together into an angry pattern of sound.

It had all taken place in this very house.

In those days—time of the first King Charles, Wyn had said—there would be far fewer other noises to distract, no trains or cars, no planes overhead, no radio, no sound of machinery; voices and the clip-clop of horses' hooves were just about all that you *could* hear.

At last I fell asleep, and instantly began to dream about Joshua Harkin—I knew it must be he, because of his gray beard and angry eyes—he stood by the coping of a well with his dog Bellman beside him, and he was shouting furiously, "Why is there no water? Why have you drawn me no water, lazy slut?" The dog was big and black, a kind of retriever; it bared its teeth and barked, accompanying Joshua's shouts with brief savage bursts of sound, while he stared angrily into the pail, rattled the well handle, and shouted again, "Why is there no water? Fetch me water, I say!"

The shouting woke me, and I found myself staring into the surprised face of Trudl, who was just stooping to turn out my light.

"Oh, it's you," I said, confused. "What time is it?"

"Eleven o'clock. What a noise you were making."

She carried a coffee cup and saucer; the spoon clinked as she put it down to pick up my book, which had fallen to the floor.

I said, "Perhaps that was what I thought was a well handle rattling. Is there a well in the garden?"

"A well? Not that I know of," said Trudl. "You were dreaming. Go to sleep again."

She switched out my light.

"Did you manage to get help for your friends while you were in London?" I asked, hoping to delay her.

Mrs. Butcher had told me that Trudl's errand in London was to visit an agency who helped refugees to leave Europe and come to England. "There's somebody as she'd like to 'elp, same as your Dad 'elped 'er. Only it ain't so easy when it's a man."

"I have no idea," said Trudl shortly. Was she annoyed that Mrs. Butcher had gossiped about her? She picked up her cup again—I could tell from the rattle —and walked away, tap-tap across the bare study floor. Up the four steps, and then the study light went out, plunging me into darkness like thick black wool. And Trudl hadn't asked me a single thing about my first day at school, I thought, injured; Mamm would have wanted to know every tiny detail. Oh, Mamm! The thought of how totally Mamm would disapprove of almost everything I had done for the past seven hours threw me into a dreadful state of misery. Reading lurid thrillers, listening to what she would have called "silly ghost stories," not doing my school preparation—I was supposed to learn a poem, I suddenly recalled. Well, I would recite *Kubla Khan,* which I already knew. . . .

Drowsily I repeated, "But O that deep romantic chasm which slanted, Down the green hill athwart a cedarn cover. . . . And 'mid this tumult Kubla heard from far, Ancestral voices prophesying war!" And, repeating it, I fell asleep again.

Chapter Three

"CHILD, you look pale and tired," said Miss Lucy, giving us a Scripture lesson next morning. She was talking about Saul and Damascus; I found it hard to pay attention.

Miss Lucy was the smallest of the three sisters, small, plump and chinless, with scanty white hair and gold-rimmed glasses that slipped continually down her nose. I liked her, but Saul's actions didn't interest me; I kept wondering about Joshua Harkin and his black dog Bellman. Where would the dog have slept? In a kennel in the garden? I hated dogs, and feared them. The thought of a dog padding about the house, specially at nighttime, was intolerable. . . .

"Did ye not sleep well?" asked Miss Lucy solici-
tously.

"I can't remember," I said with truth. But I knew
that my sleep had been punctuated all the way by
flickering dreams—about Dracula, about the big sled
dog Buck, howling over his master's grave, about
Patty and Ralph, escaping over the Channel to
France. And then coming back again. . . .

" 'And, as he journeyed, he came near Damascus,' " read Miss Lucy. "Sit up straight, now, Julia
dear, and pay attention. 'And he fell to earth, and
heard a voice saying to him—' "

I wondered what Patty had looked like. What
might she have been wearing when she came running out, summoned by her father's furious shout:
"Why is there no water? Bring me water, I say!"

"*What* did you say, my dear?" inquired Miss Lucy
gently, in surprise, turning from the blackboard,
where she had been chalking the relative positions of
Damascus and Jerusalem, in a map of the Holy Land.

"I—I don't think I said anything, Miss Lucy—"

Tim turned on me round eyes of astonishment.

"Perhaps it was a sneeze," said Miss Lucy in kind
reproof. "When you sneeze, you know, dear, you
should always say, 'Excuse me.' "

"Yes—I'm sorry." I gulped confusedly. But I knew
that I had not spoken. Where, then, had the voice
come from? There had certainly been a voice. Miss
Lucy gave me another extremely doubtful glance as
she ended the Scripture lesson.

"Maybe ye had best lie down for a wee minute
during break, childie? Or would ye run home and see

what your mother thinks? Ye could take the afternoon off from school if ye're not feeling quite the thing?"

"My stepmother. No, no, thank you—truly, I'm all right."

"Ye're so *pale*, child—"

"I'm just naturally pale," I explained, "because of having red hair."

Trudl, I was certain, would not be in the least pleased to have me back for the rest of the day. She had made no secret, after breakfast, of her eagerness to get me out of the house and have it to herself.

"Can you throw your voice?" Tim asked me in break, when, having eaten our biscuits, we were idly tossing a ball back and forth in the tiny paved yard.

"Throw my *voice*?" Startled, I threw him the ball.

"You know—ventri-whatsit. Ventrilockism," said Tim. "When a person makes his voice come from somewhere else. What people do with puppets. Making them seem to be talking."

"Oh, that. No, I can't." The ball had slipped from my fingers, and I had to follow it out into Chapel Passage.

"Come along, come along in, children!" floated the voice of Miss Sybil from the little school building. "Break time's over."

"Well, that was what it sounded like," said Tim, as we walked to the door.

"Was what sounded like?"

"That queer voice. Coming from your stomach. A sort of croak."

"I don't know what you're *talking* about!"

Huffily I pushed the ball at him, and walked into the classroom.

While Miss Sybil taught us a few French verbs I kept my teeth clenched together, and my mind clenched upon what she was saying. *"Je suis, tu es, il est . . ."*

Did Patty and Ralph know any French? How ever did they manage, when they crossed the Channel to get married? Did people learn French at school in those days?

AFTER SCHOOL that afternoon Tim asked, rather shyly, if he might come back to my house for an hour or so; his mother was going home earlier than usual (she taught at the Grammar School) and had said she would pick him up at five.

"Where's she going to pick you up?"

"At the Land Gate."

Where Ralph's aunt lived, I remembered.

"Well, then, let's go and play in the Gun Gardens."

"All right," he said, but his face fell. I guessed he had wanted to get a look at the inside of Harken House.

"The thing is," I explained, "my stepmother is working and she doesn't like to be disturbed."

But just as we reached the Gun Gardens it began to rain—a cold, penetrating May rain—so rather reluctantly I said I supposed he could come back to the house, and we walked across Church Square and down Harbor Hill.

"Aren't you lucky to live in a haunted house," Tim said in an awestruck voice as I opened the front door.

"Well, I haven't seen any ghost," I said shortly.

When I took him up to my room he seemed a bit

disappointed. "I thought it would all be much darker and weirder," he said.

"Who's there?" called a voice, and Trudl appeared, looking rather put out, with a carbon-paper smudge on her forehead, and an inkblot on her finger. "Oh, it's you," she said flatly; I wondered who she had expected.

"This is Tim Bellyap, from school," I said. "He's waiting to meet his mother at five."

"I see. All right." She turned away, then said, over her shoulder, "Do you want some biscuits, or something?"

"Yes, please."

"On the kitchen dresser. In the red tin with George V."

The kitchen at Harken House was a shadowy, gloomy room with dark blue linoleum on the floor and a sharp metallic smell from the coke slowly roasting in the huge old boiler which growled and sighed all day and spewed out fumes. The kitchen window looked straight on to a gray area wall, topped by the tangle of mint on the skyline. As soon as we had helped ourselves to three biscuits apiece (captain's biscuits, they were; very plain) I said, "Come on, let's go up to the attic."

Tim liked the ladder, and at least up there it was light. And I could show him my pile of paperbacks, since I had nothing else to show.

But Tim was no reader. Though he liked the picture of the White Worm, he didn't seem interested in the books. He wanted, I found, to talk about Joshua Harkin.

"There was a mayor of Dune lived in this house once, and *he* saw him. He knew it was Joshua."

"How?"

"He was a tall man in a brown robe, like a monk's, and a short beard. He said, 'My daughter killed me. I shan't rest until I have proper burial.' And something about a curse."

"Oh, surely Patty didn't kill him?" I said, shocked. "Her own *father*?"

"He'd killed her husband," pointed out Tim.

"That's only what people say. He might have died of the plague."

"And Joshua used to make Patty look in the glass and foretell the future."

"Did he? How do you know?"

"Somebody told my father that."

"What kind of glass?"

"I dunno."

"Why did he make her do that?"

Tim thought. "Not sure. Maybe he got too old to do it himself. Or lost the knack. Scrying, it was called. Then he wouldn't let her marry Ralph."

"That's true. . . ."

The attics were the only rooms in Harken House that still had patterned wallpaper. I had asked Trudl why this was and she told me, "Oh, there were wallpapers in all the rooms once, but Gerald had them scraped off. He hates patterns. But he never bothered about the attics."

Now, curled up on the attic floor, staring at the slope of the ceiling, I agreed with Gerald. This pattern was a small, intricate in-and-out design of reddish-pink tendrils on a paler pink background and

I hated it. If you looked at it for more than a minute or two, you began to see the eyes and faces of little creatures in among the leaves and sprays, hiding, peering out. How could my brother Joe have stood them, when he slept up here? I was tremendously glad that Trudl hadn't put me up here, despite that nighttime walk through the dark study.

"Is there a cellar in this house?" asked Tim, tiring of the books.

"Yes," I said reluctantly. Anyway, it was too wet to go out on the roof.

"Let's go down there," he said with shining eyes.

"Why? Oh, all right."

We went downstairs again, tiptoeing past Trudl's workroom door, from which came a tap of typewriter and smell of cigarette smoke.

On the first-floor landing, a wide wooden ledge ran out between the wall and the stair, where I had first encountered Trudl; Tim ran daringly, expertly, out along this ledge, then dropped the six feet down to the stairs below, breaking his fall by catching the banister rail as he landed. His run, his spring, his drop, were done with great precision and elegance. Tim was a natural athlete. Rather clumsy myself, I knew I couldn't possibly hope to copy this feat without falling, or failing to grab the rail in time, so I followed him sedately down the steps in the usual manner.

The cellar was underneath the dining room, reached by a door in the kitchen wall and twelve stone steps. On its gritty floor lay a heap of coke for the boiler, coal for fires, a drum of kerosene, kindling, and old pieces of discarded furniture. One wall contained a fireplace and a brick oven.

"I expect this was the kitchen once," said Tim, prowling about.

I thought of Patty peeling potatoes here.

"And, look, this bricked-up arch must have led to the cellar next door. My dad says lots of the cellars in Dune opened into each other; because of all the smuggling, you know. I wonder if there's a well under this floor. He says they had wells in cellars sometimes. If I had a hazel twig I'd dowse for it."

I didn't ask what *dowse* meant; suddenly I had had more than enough of Tim and wished that he would leave. Perhaps he caught my thought. He exclaimed, "Lummy, there's five striking. I'll have to run, or Mum will twist my ears."

Much relieved, I saw him out of the front door and settled down to write the story of St. Paul on the kitchen table; although dark there, it was warmer than upstairs.

The boiler squeaked and creaked; a bird with a harsh voice chattered angrily in the little courtyard garden, and from somewhere in the house came a low regular buzz. It sounded like the dial tone of a telephone. But of course there was no telephone in Harken House. In those days only rich people had telephones.

That night in bed, after Trudl's cheese omelette, and a shallow, chilly bath, grudgingly trickled out by the huge copper geyser, I fell asleep fast and began to dream at once.

I was in a half-finished room; one wall was still in skeleton stage, oak upright beams, the gaps between them not yet filled in. Beyond this partition, only dimly seen, two people were arguing at the tops of their voices.

"Listen to me. *Listen,* will you! What I tell you is the truth! I am learned, I *know.* There is a bad hair on your head, and it wants to harm you. It *will* harm you, believe me, if it is allowed to have its way. It must be pulled out—dragged out—rooted out!"

"I don't believe you! You only tell me that to frighten me—to make me do what you want—"

The younger voice was shrill, hysterical in its defiance.

"I don't believe you, I *won't* believe you—"

Beyond the speakers, and unseen by them, three shapes were watching, three veiled figures seated under a kind of canopy of spiderweb. Two of them had eyes visible, above their veils; the third was completely wrapped but in spite of this an icy-cold feeling of malignity came from her—

I woke myself out of that one by shouting aloud, and realized that both of the voices had been issuing from my own throat. While asleep, I had reared myself up and was crouched on my pillow, clutching the iron bed-rail. My hands shook, my throat was sore from shouting. When I switched on the bedside light, I found that only ten minutes had passed since I switched it off. Now I felt totally wide awake; it did not seem possible that I could ever sleep again. I would have to read. But, as I could not face the trip across the dark study and up the ladder to the attic for another paperback, I was obliged to fall back on *Dr. Faustus.*

It was about how he sold his soul to the devil.

Chapter Four

"HOW ARE ALD, SKALD, AND BALD?" inquired a post-card from Gerald; it had Mont Blanc on the picture side in turquoise-blue and ice-white. "Give my love to the ladies—and to you, too, dearie."

That was all. Trudl had presumably read it, for it lay, written side up, at my breakfast place next to the boiled egg. She made no comment on it.

"Did he send you one too?" I asked tactlessly; she shook her head. Today she seemed out of spirits, and said nothing as I plowed through the egg, doing my best to make it less disgusting by dipping in pieces of toast.

I wondered if Trudl minded the fact that Gerald

didn't seem to write to her much. Did she love him? Or had the marriage really been nothing but a business arrangement? I had no knowledge about love between grown people, how it might be displayed; my mother and stepfather kept a cool, if friendly, distance between them, and my early memories came to a stop before the time when Mamm and Gerald were married and living here in this house; he had left her long before he took up with Trudl and there had been several other people in between. When Mamm referred to Gerald it was in very dry terms. So, love to me was a foreign language.

Like a picture, I thought, that you don't understand.

"He doesn't say anything here about when he might be coming back. Do you think it will be soon?"

"I have no idea. I told you that already," Trudl answered crossly, and getting up, began to stack the plates and cups. "Run along, or you will be late for school."

Summer was beginning to warm up now, May moving toward June. I had been away from home for three weeks, almost four, had written home twice and received three letters from Mamm. "I hope you are remembering to wash your hair," she wrote. "Do let me know if you need any more clothes. I wonder if Gerald is back from Switzerland yet? Have you been to the beach often? I expect you are having a nice time with Mrs. Demarest."

I did not feel this was true. Trudl, more and more, seemed bored and irritated by my company. We saw little of each other, save at meals. Either she would be up in her workroom, where she spent long hours writing, or she was out of the house, I seldom knew where. Sometimes Wyn or Mrs. Butcher were there to keep me company. Sometimes I invited Tim in, or we flew homemade kites on the Town Salts, or climbed on the logs in the Shipyard, or scrambled up and down the more accessible bits of the town cliff. Once or twice I had been to Tim's house. Both his parents taught at the grammar school and they had a small untidy bungalow in the village of Ramsden, a mile out of Dune. They were kind, busy people, with scant time to spare for either Tim or me.

Sometimes I felt that nobody noticed me at all. I was obliged to hang on to myself, as a traveler hangs on to his wallet in a foreign town; everything around me seemed to be sliding into an ungraspable mist, with myself in the middle, out of reach of everybody.

"Seen your ghost yet, have you?" Mr. Bellyap would sometimes absently ask me. But he never waited for an answer. He had a sailor's beard, and a deep, impressive, baying voice, yet he never waited for anybody's answer. I could see why Tim was so slow, vague, and dreamy; nobody at his home ever paid the least heed to anything he had to say. So he had given up trying.

His parents did, though, kindly take Tim and me to Mayfield's circus, which turned up late in May and set up its big top on the Town Salts. I had never been to a circus in my life and was thrilled by the liberty horses, the bareback riders, the ladies in their spangles, the acrobats, the loud, brassy music, and the lion tamer cracking a fourteen-foot lash at his roaring, raging charges. By the end of the show I felt wholly uplifted, transported.

"Enjoyed it, did you?"

"Oh yes! It was *wonderful!*"

"That's right. That's right. Good night, then!" called Mr. Bellyap, starting up his little three-wheeler Morgan car. "Don't need us to see you home, do you?"

"Of course not. Good night!" I called. "And thank you!"

But, walking among the rest of the crowd, diagonally across the Salts to the foot of the steps that would take me back up the cliff and into the town, I had a sudden piercingly strange and menacing experience. There was a large burned patch in the grass, where, I suppose, the circus people had had a bonfire; picking my way across this I was all at once aware of a hoarse, grinding voice, which was shouting: "No! NO! I am not to be burned! I am not to be burned! It is not in my stars! I shall confound you all yet!"

Startled, I looked all around me—then realized, with a sick feeling of shock and amazement, that the voice had come from inside *myself*—I could still feel the vibration of it in my rib cage. Luckily nobody else had noticed; people in the crowd were chattering and laughing and singing. Thank heaven for that!

Breathless, panting, with sobs of fright, I hurled myself up the zigzag flights of steps, along Church Street and Rope Walk, down Harbor Hill, and so home.

Trudl, for a wonder, was in. (More and more often, nowadays, she would be absent after supper, at choir practice, giving German lessons, playing chess with an elderly lady. "Your father left me with very little money, so I must support myself somehow," she had

said, curtly, when I asked if she enjoyed playing chess
with the old lady. This made me feel bad and I tried to
eat less at mealtimes.)

"Did you enjoy the circus?" she asked, putting her
head out of her workroom as I ran gasping up the
stairs.

"Oh, yes—thank you—it was lovely." Immensely
relieved at finding her in for once, I made no mention
of the thing that had happened to me; in any case,
what could I have said? It was like hearing a loud-
speaker in the street and then discovering that your
own voice came out of the megaphone. No, not that,
because the voice, the words that exploded from my
breastbone were *not* my own voice, *not* my own
words; that was the particular horror. It was like having a hideous worm shoot its narrow head out of your
eye, or a rat unexpectedly, gruesomely, appear out of
your stomach. I felt invaded, made use of, helpless.

"Well," said Trudl, "good! Sweet dreams, then."
And she went back into her workroom, closing the
door. She kept a little radio in there, and through the
thin door, I suddenly heard the voice of Adolf Hitler
snarl out, nasal and resonant, like wickedness made
audible. Had those been the marks of tears on Trudl's
cheeks, I wondered, as I groped my way across the
dark study to my bedroom door.

That night I had a dream about a little, odd-
shaped house, with seven outside doors, which I was
frantically trying to make weatherproof against a
lashing storm; as fast as I closed doors and windows,
and plugged holes, the wind and the rain found their
way in through other weak spots, through cracks and
chinks all over the house. I kept listening for a voice

which I expected to tell me what to do, but no voice could be heard. I am deaf, I thought despairingly, that's what the real trouble is, I have gone deaf; which was ridiculous because, while the lightning flashed, I could hear the thunder crackle and peal; I woke with huge relief to find a real storm raging and real rain sliding in rods over my dark-gray skylight.

ARITHMETIC was my least favorite subject at school. I had made very little sense of it when learning with Mamm, and did hardly better now with Miss Sybil; so it seemed in keeping with this dismal day, and after a frightening night, that the eldest Norn should leave Tim and me alone in our small room, with the rain battering our narrow pointed window and a one-hour test in multiplication and long division.

Tim applied himself silently and doggedly; he was slow, but nearly always got his answers right in the end. Whereas I dashed at the hateful problems, scribbled out a mess of unlikely-looking answers, then sat staring at my untidy sheets of paper in a wretched state of mind.

Was this, I wondered, how madness began? Hearing other people's loud angry voices coming out of one's own mouth? Would I have to be locked up, like old Mrs. Canning at home, who shouted abuse at passersby over her garden fence and was at last taken off to the county asylum? Would I become like the father in *Hans Brinker* who, after a head injury, was out of his wits for twelve years? And tried to burn his wife in the fire?

Miss Sybil looked at me in a troubled way as she went through my papers, correcting them and trying to show me where I had gone wrong. This time she did not mention Trudl, but asked if my father were still away from home. I said yes, and explained about the play translated into German being put on at Lucerne.

"Your father is a very brilliant playwright, my dear," she said. "It is a great privilege to have such a gifted father."

"Yes," I agreed glumly.

"Do ye think that ye'd like to write plays, too, one day, perhaps?"

"No," I surprised myself by replying, "I want to be a fireman."

"A *fireman*? Good heavens, child, they don't have women firemen." She brushed aside the idea and went on, "It must be very interesting for your father to hear his work translated into a foreign language. Does he speak German himself, I wonder?"

Fairly well, I told her; he had visited Germany for quite long periods.

"Has it ever occurred to you that the wonderful thing about mathematics is that it does not need to be translated?" suggested Miss Sybil, surprising me very much. "Anybody can read and understand an example of multiplication or division, if they are English, French or—or Eskimo. Isn't that amusing! Numbers are international—like art and music. You can look at a picture or hear a tune in any language."

"That's true." I pondered this interesting fact for a moment or two, then argued, "Their names aren't international, though. Numbers, I mean. It's only when you see the problem written down. Not when you hear it. In French one is *'un'* and two is *'deux'*—if a Frenchman told me how to do the sum, I wouldn't understand."

Tim looked up from his desk, his honest forehead corrugated with earnest thought. He might have been going to say, "Julia doesn't seem to understand the sum even when you explain it in English, Miss Sybil." He did come out with these down-to-earth remarks sometimes. Hastily I went on, "Miss Sybil, is there anywhere in Dune where I might be able to see a picture of Joshua Harkin, who used to live in my father's house?"

She shook her head at me, bothered and startled.

"Eh, now, why in the wide world would ye want to see a picture of *him*, my dear?"

"Oh, we just thought we'd like to find out a bit more about him, and see what he looked like, didn't we, Tim?"

"Umn," said Tim.

"Well—to tell ye the truth, child, I don't know. I've no idea. But—let me think now—Miss Enthoven at the Rochelle Library—she might be able to help ye."

Trudl had shown me this little library, in a lane off Market Street, paid for by a charitable trust founded by Huguenots who had escaped from France and lived in Dune three hundred years ago. I had gone in there and looked around but decided that it was a total loss. There were no children's books on its shelves, and those for adults, in thick brown bindings, were all at least fifty years old. They smelled of long-since-smoked cigarettes, crumbling mothballs, and cups of cold tea. I had picked one off the shelf, attracted by its title, *Red Cotton Nightcap Country*, but gave up in despair and put it back. It had not struck me that the library might have other things besides novels.

"Well," said Miss Sybil with a sigh, "ye and I must have another talk about your sums, child. Ye do seem to have a wee problem there." She handed Tim back his sheets with the rare smile that she kept for him specially— "Well done, my boy!" and we passed on to English grammar, at which I shone and Tim floundered in total confusion. (It was true that I could not see the *point* of grammar, but at least it was easy to foretell the answers, simply from the sound of the words.)

"Did you hear Hitler last night, Miss Sybil?" I asked her, as a distraction from parsing. "My stepmother was listening to him. She says he is going to take a piece of Czechoslovakia."

"*That* evil man? No, indeed I did not," she said briskly. "I make a point of switching off, if ever his voice comes on the air. And if your stepmother were wise, she would do the same. It is like taking poison into one's ear."

". . . *Not* a good example for the children, I very much fear!" she was saying to Miss Lucy half an hour later, in break, when I passed their cubbyhole door. "Encouraging them in all sorts of morbid fancies of a most pernicious kind. Do ye know what that child is reading, Lucy? Dr. Faustus. *Dr. Faustus!* Of all the unsuitable works!"

"A very unfortunate environment," Miss Lucy mumbled through her digestive biscuit.

I sighed, thinking how much *more* unsuitable Miss Sybil would find *Dracula* or *The Lair of the White*

Worm. But Sunnyhay School had no room for a library
in its tiny building; there was a single shelf of *John
and Mary* readers, all of which I had whizzed through
long ago.

At the end of the day Miss Sybil beckoned to me
and said, "Here, my love, I have written this wee note
to Miss Enthoven; we'll see if she can be of any help to
ye in yer searches. But mind! I think it would be far
and away better if you and Tim played more out of
doors instead of filling yer heads with these old matters, which are probably best left alone. So—"

"Oh, but we do play out of doors," I assured her.
"When it's not raining like today we play in the Shipyard and the Gun Gardens—"

"So," continued Miss Sybil, gently silencing me
with a wave of the hand and a reproving shake of the
head, "so I have written off for two nice wee airplanes
for the two of ye; a special offer they have just now for
six tops from packets of Rice Flakes, which my sisters
and I eat for breakfast every day."

"Oh, Miss Sybil, thank you, that's *very* kind of
you—"

"Frog models!" she ended impressively.

I was impressed; Frog models were, at that time,
the best of their kind.

"Now run along with ye; don't waste too much
time burrowing about in the Rochelle Library—but a
nice game of bat-and-ball, now, or a nice brisk
walk—"

Tim, however, was due for a piano lesson in
Church Square, so, after giving him the news of the
two nice little airplanes, which he received with utter
astonishment— "Why in the world would the old girl

do that?"—I went off by myself to the library. It was housed in a single room in a tall cobble-built house, part of what had once been a monastery, entered by a flight of outside steps.

Miss Enthoven the librarian was mouselike, with pale blinking eyes and smooth white hair, and was also, as I soon found out, almost totally deaf.

"Hmmn, now, history of Harken House," she murmured, after reading Miss Sybil's note, shuffled away, and presently returned with a small aged leather-bound volume. *A History of the Town of Dune,* it was called, *Its Worthies, Its Curiosities & Various Antiquities, compiled by a Doctor of Divinity.* The book contained, I found, a whole chapter about Mansions and Private Houses of Some Interest. "May I take it home?" I asked Miss Enthoven.

My question had to be repeated three times, each time in a louder voice, before she finally heard me. Then she laid her finger on her lips, glancing at an elderly couple who were in the library, a man and a woman, both reading magazines. Shaking her head— "No, no, my love, the book is too valuable. It is, you see, our only copy—very rare. Very few of our books may be lent. You must read it here. Now, I'll just see if I can find . . ."

She trotted off again into a back room and I heard boxes being moved about. Meanwhile I sat myself down at a table—there were two or three small ones —and studied the *History of Dune.* It was illustrated here and there with little smudgy black line drawings, of buildings mostly. There was no picture of Harken House, but a reproduction of Joshua's memorial slab over the front door.

For the first time it occurred to me to wonder where Joshua was buried.

"Thisse building," said the section on Harken House, "was first erected as a granarye and store-house in the yeare 1616 by Jasper Harkin, a seed merchant and forage dealer. He prospered and his sonne Joshua was a man of some education, at first destined for ye Church. . . ." Poring over the crabbed text I learned that Joshua Harkin studied mathematics at Cambridge, and went on to read philosophy, medicine, and disputation at Heidelberg; then, after some trouble (not specified) he returned to his native town, married, and set up as a doctor and general consultant. But his wife died young "and it began to be rumored about the towne that in queste of more knowledge, for whiche he hadde a deep thyrste, he had sould his soul to the Evil One (by setting his bloode in a saucer of warm ashes). And, therebye, his desyre for Learning and Power was—during the space of twenty-one years—amply granted by his Devilish Master."

Just like Faustus! I thought. But wasn't it rather queer that, if Joshua really had all this knowledge and power, he wouldn't travel about the world, as Faustus did, to Rome and such places, but just stayed quietly in Dune?

The book went briefly into the story of Joshua's daughter and the apprentice Ralph. "Soe, Ralph being deade and the townspeople persuaded this Fatality was broughte aboutt by Joshua's evil artes, they purposed to burn himm for a Wizard. Hee, however, escaping them (by magicall means, some sedde) fled to his House & therein barricaded himselfe. And manye were wishful to set fyre to the house & himme inne yt, but a neighbour, knowing a privye way into his cellar, the housse was thusse entered but found to be emptye; nor, indeed, was Joshua ever seene or hearde of from that time forward. Moste, however, were of the opinion that hee had been spirited away to Hell by his Dark Master. And thisse writer has been able to come at no history of what became of his daughter Patience, though some sedde shee had taken her father's life in revenge for that of her younge Husband."

So that's where Tim's father got the story, I thought, closing the book. But if Patty killed him, where was the body? And where was she? Wasn't it more likely that Joshua escaped through the neighbor's cellar before the angry townspeople arrived?

Miss Enthoven returned with a dusty black folder filled with old yellow engravings and prints.

"Somewhere among these," she whispered in her thin, thready voice— "ah, yes, here it is, I knew it was in here somewhere"—and she fished out a black-and-white engraving of a man with an angry intent face, wearing a black hat, clutching a scroll. *Joshua Harkin, Gent.,* said the caption under it, in flowing italics.

"It must have been taken from a picture, do you see—" Miss Enthoven was beginning, when the elderly man called to her.

"Miss Enthoven!"—in a voice loud enough to attract her attention— "Miss Enthoven, can you help me a moment? Do you know where the issue before this has got to?"

"Ah, now, just a moment, Mr. Redditch—I believe

it might be with Canon Cawley's papers"—and she pattered away.

I went on staring at the face of Joshua Harkin. It was an immensely powerful, concentrated face—the lips pursed together, slightly protruding, the brows lowered, with vertical creases between them. The hand that grasped the scroll was crunching it flat. Curls of darkish grizzled hair were dimly visible beyond his hollow cheeks. He had no beard. He wore a fur coat with a high collar over some kind of plain gathered white shirt, and the gleam of a silver ring could just be seen on his wedding finger. The harder I looked at him, the harder I found it to *stop* looking. What color had his eyes been? Dark brown, perhaps; dark, anyway; their piercing stare went right past me, right over my shoulder, and fixed on something out of sight behind me. Vaguely I remembered the command, *Vade retro, Satanas,* Get thee behind me, Satan, and thought how unpleasant it would be to have Satan behind one's back, doing something horrible and unseen; better by far to have him in front, visible, and at least know what he was about.

Still, after all, nobody had actually proved that Joshua sold his soul to the devil. It was only what people said about him, because he knew more than his neighbors?

All of a sudden, as I sat, almost mesmerized, with my eyes fixed on those of the portrait, I felt an ache in my ribs, beginning as a faint pinpoint of pain, but rapidly growing to a fierce heat that seemed likely to burst my breastbone into splinters; and then, out of me, roared a voice which had nothing whatever to do with me—a hoarse voice, resentful, strong, combative: *"Why must I be daily pestered by these odious fools?"*

Aghast at what had happened I glanced in terror about the room. But the old lady reader had just departed, tottering through the door clutching her beaded cloth bag; the old gentleman was in the storeroom with Miss Enthoven hunting for the journal that had been misplaced; and, at the precise moment of my outburst, it chanced that a pneumatic drill had started up its row on the cobbled hill outside, where a trench was being dug for a gas main; nobody had heard me. *Nobody?* I thought, my teeth literally chattering with terror; how could I possibly tell that nobody heard? If there are voices that speak suddenly out of nowhere, there must also be unseen ears, all around us, wherever we go—listening?

With hands that shook like wires in a wind, I gathered my school things together, closed the *History of Dune,* placed it on top of Joshua's picture, and walked unsteadily to the door.

"Good-bye, Miss Enthoven—thank you!" I called, in a thin, dried-up voice that seemed no more my own than the other one had been. No answer came. Miss Enthoven probably didn't hear me. But I could not bear to wait in that room for another moment, and hurled myself down the outside staircase so fast that I tripped, and almost landed with a broken leg on the cobbles below.

Would Trudl be at home? I wondered, as I ran along the High Street. I could hardly bear to think of the house empty and waiting for me.

Trudl was not at home but—to my mixed relief and impatience—Wyn was there, pimply and chatty, with a bag of Bassett's licorice allsorts. A little of Wyn went a long way, I had decided, and time spent with her was rather boringly wasted—but today I was glad of anybody who would help to keep my mind off what had happened.

It was a fine warm evening and we sat in the garden with cups of mint tea and the sweets.

> "Oh—the king's hor-ses, [sang Wyn, out of
>   tune]
> *And*—the king's men,
> Marched up the hill and they marched down
>   again;
> The king's hor-ses; *and* the king's men.
> They don't go—to meet the foe—
> You might think so—but oh, dear, no—"

"Shall I tell your fortune, Jule?" she broke off singing to say.

"All right." I was not enthusiastic, but it was better than her singing.

She told our fortunes in tea leaves, reversing the teacups and inspecting the tea leaves at the bottom.

My fortune showed me flying through the air—according to Wyn.

"You *can* learn to fly, you know," said Wyn. "Here's how: you have to steal a bit of earth from somebody else's garden, without asking for it, and bury it in a seashell, with some rose petals and a silver button; then you go to sleep, three nights running, saying, 'I want to have wings,' three times over. Get it? Three nights running, and three times each night. Then the wings will grow, you'll see!" She gazed at me, poker faced, the corners of her mouth solemnly drawn down.

Even I was not gullible enough to believe that I could grow wings, though I passionately wished to, and my mind did race off in spite of me: where could I steal a bit of earth—perhaps from the Sunnyhay hydrangea tubs? And the shell, the rose petals, the silver button? Where in the world could I find a silver button? Aloud I said, "It can't be as easy as that, or everyone would have wings."

Wyn had brought a dream book with her—a thin, thumbed dog-eared pamphlet, greasy from years of family use.

"What did you dream about last night? A house— let's see. A house could mean that some money is coming to you soon. Or that you are going to get married. You! Fancy!" She giggled, and put her hand over her mouth. "Now, *I* was dreaming last night about a monkey—let's see what a monkey means."

She turned to the letter *M.* Meanly, I wondered if she had invented the monkey dream; why should Wyn dream about a monkey, for heaven's sake?

"Monkey!" read Wyn triumphantly. "A handsome stranger will soon come into your life—that's true, dreams always go by opposites, they say—bringing new poss—poss—possibilities. What's a possibility, Jule, d'you think?"

"Perhaps he'll offer you a job in the films. Perhaps he'll take you to Hollywood."

Hollywood was Wyn's mirage, far over the horizon. Twice a week she went to the new film at the Dune Picture Palace, and then, next day, told me what it had been about. I could not afford to go as I had only tenpence left of Mamm's ten shillings; the money had dribbled away on I knew not what—chocolate drops, hair grips, a cheap fountain pen.

"Go on! Hollywood!" said Wyn derisively; but she was pleased, just the same.

She sang:

> "Oh, they're tough, mighty tough, in the West
> They've got little curly hay-ers on their
>   chest—"

"Wyn," I asked, cutting off this tedious song, one of my least favorites in her repertoire, "Did you ever hear that Joshua Harkin had sold his soul to the devil?"

"No, I did not! Mum says there's no such thing as the devil," Wyn said, looking nervously behind her at the garden wall, "and you didn't ought to mention him, it's bad luck. Let's play beggar-my-neighbor."

She brought out a limp pack of cards from her skirt pocket and we played beggar-my-neighbor on the little iron garden table for an interminable time, with the luck of the game wandering pointlessly back and forth between us. Beggar-my-neighbor is a terribly tiresome game between two players and I began to yawn and think about my schoolwork, still to be done; the dreadful occurrence in the library seemed a long time ago, and perhaps I had imagined it; perhaps it had happened to a different *I*, not this one sitting here slapping at midges.

"Let's tell our fortunes with the cards now," proposed Wyn, yawning also, scraping all the pack together and expertly shuffling. "Dad's sister, my auntie

Blossom, taught me how." And she dealt out twelve cards into a circle, then set three in the middle.

"Now you put down three—north, east, and west."

"Why?" I asked, obeying.

"Why? I dunno why. That's the way it's done, that's all. Now, three in the middle. Now, pick one from the middle of the pack, and take north."

North turned out to be the king of spades. Wyn's mouth dropped open. She said hastily, "Perhaps I made a mis—" and the voice burst out of me again.

"Enough of this mummery! Bailzybub is not mocked. Look in the glass, my daughter, look in the glass. Only so may the clouds of dark be dispersed."

"My stars!" gulped Wyn, after a moment or two. She had turned pale with shock—even paler than her normal pasty color. "My stars, Jule, was that *you?* Saying that? In that funny voice? Was that *you?*"

I was sick and quivering with dread. I ought to have said, "I don't know! I need help! I don't know what to do!"

Instead, after taking several deep breaths, I told her, "It's called throwing your voice. Don't you know about it? People do it on the stage."

"Coo," said Wyn doubtfully. "It didn't sound a bit like you. Can you do it again?"

"Not just now."

"Who's Bailzy-whatsit—when he's at home?"

"Just a name."

Trudl came into the garden. "Oh, hallo," she said to Wyn without much enthusiasm, and to me, "I brought some fish-and-chips for supper. Do you want to run and wash your hands?"

Taking the hint, Wyn said, "I better be on me way, then. Mum wanted chips too." (A fish-and-chip van with a stinking, black-fuming chimney made the tour of the town once a week. A packet of chips cost a penny.)

I washed my hands at the kitchen sink, dejectedly inspecting my black fingernails. I could imagine Mamm at my shoulder saying, "My goodness! You run upstairs to the bathroom, right away, and brush those awful nails before you come to supper. And just look at your hair! When did you wash it last? It isn't even properly combed."

Trudl never seemed to notice my hair or nails, or how often I changed my blouse. At least she never commented. Mamm's imagined, reproachful voice followed me about, most of the day, at this time, and made me feel dreadfully guilty, but without influencing what I actually did. So I felt a great deal of sympathy with Dr. Faustus. *His* good angel kept following about, crying, "Repent! Repent! It still isn't too late!" But Faustus could never pull himself together enough to follow this sensible advice. The end of the play about Faustus was terrifying, with adders and serpents carrying him off to hell. I wished I hadn't read it, and resolved to try *The Duchess of Malfi* next. That one seemed to start harmlessly enough.

After supper, and after I had tried to do my sums, I crept upstairs to bed. Trudl was in her room working. I could not remember feeling so tired, ever before, in my whole life. I thought how wonderful it would be suddenly to find myself at home, in my own small close-fitting bed, with Joe and Anna back for the holidays, Mamm and Anna chatting in the kitchen,

Joan Aiken

Joe and my stepfather playing Haydn duets on the piano, my little brother singing in his cot. . . .

The idea comforted me, and I slept. No voice came that night to trouble me, or any dream. But in the morning I had a vague memory that once in the night, when my right hand chanced to dangle over the side of the bed, something ice-cold and wet had touched it.

Chapter Five

TIM ASKED ME in break next day how I had got on at
the library, and was soberly excited to hear that Miss
Enthoven had actually been able to produce a picture
of Joshua Harkin.

"Did he look like a wizard? I'd like to see him.
Let's go back after school and take another look."

This suggestion filled me with fright. Suppose the
voice burst out of me again at sight of the picture?
Miss Enthoven might not notice, but Tim certainly
would; and I did not think that he would be fobbed off
by the sort of explanation that I had given to Wyn.
Tim might be slow of speech, but he was not at all
stupid.

"You go and look at it," I said. "I'll wait for you in the cliff garden. I don't think Miss Enthoven would be pleased if too many of us keep going in and bothering her."

"Oh," he said. "I hadn't thought of that. Do you really think she'd mind? All right, I'll go."

We walked together to the cliff gardens, and I settled myself there, sitting on a low brick wall in the warm sun, while Tim went on round to the Rochelle Library.

The cliff gardens were a long narrow strip of rockeries and rose beds, with benches and a paved walk, which lay along the top of the north cliff, and looked down to the Town Salts below, where a cricket match was now taking place. The drop down, here, was steep and fairly sheer, with the road at the foot, between cliff and fields.

"Don't you lean too far over, now," scolded old Mr. Whitgift, who cared for the rose beds and did his best to discourage children from coming into his garden and climbing on his walls; the garden was meant for old people, he said, not for kids. I nodded impatiently and moved myself back an inch or two. I was thinking about that night when the people of Dune dragged Joshua Harkin down to the Salts, intending to burn him. Was there another angry crowd up here, proposing to watch the spectacle? Or were the cliff gardens not there in Joshua's day? Probably not. More likely there would have been a high town wall here then, circling round to the massive Land Gate, with its low round arch, just wide enough to take a horse and cart, but nothing much bigger. No, of course there would have been no cliff gardens at that time—

people in those days still feared that the French would invade, because they had done so, three or four times; Miss Lucy had been telling us about it. How queer it must have been, when you had every reason to expect that the wicked French might turn up, any day, with sabers and cutlasses, and eat your children; or when you believed in the devil and decided to burn your neighbor, because his son-in-law had died, and he had been angry about the marriage.

A cloud drifted across the sun, and I shivered. After all, I thought, were things any different now? There was Adolf Hitler, like a black spider, creeping across Europe, pulling his web after him, snatching country after country, no different from Attila the Hun, or Napoleon, simply because he said he hadn't enough room at home. We English thought we were perfectly safe, in our cozy island, but were we so safe? And we thought that the devil was just a folk tale, a fairy tale, no more likely than Little Red Riding Hood and the wolf—but then unexplained things happened, terrifying things, like those hideous voices bursting out of me.

What caused them?

I remembered tales of people possessed by devils in the New Testament, which Mamm and I used to read together when I was at home. There was the devil inside a man who, when asked what his name was, replied, "Our name is Legion"—a horrible thought. There were the devils who escaped and ran off into the Gadarene swine. Were devils the same as evil spirits? Was Dracula possessed by a devil, or the white worm lady? *Possessed*—what a foul word that was! I shivered again. It was like being a slave, a serf.

You did not own yourself, could not control your own actions. It was like being mad. Perhaps mad people were really possessed by devils.

Fleetingly, I considered consulting Miss Sybil about my state. But what would she do? Worry, think I was ill, have a talk with Trudl; and Trudl would be no use at all, I was quite sure of that; Trudl was too concerned with her own problems. Or perhaps Miss Sybil would write to Mamm, and I did not want that either. Poor Mamm would be dreadfully upset, and what could she do, a hundred miles off? Again, nothing.

I had never been in the habit of confiding in adults about my ills or problems. The small ones vanished, one way or another, in the end; the larger ones had always been observed by Mamm and dealt with, sometimes even before I was aware of them myself.

In Dune, it was different. Here I had so *many* worries, large and small, jumbled together—from the hateful voices, bursting out of me, down to my dirty fingernails, a bad ink-stain on my best skirt, a hole in my favorite jersey, and a mysterious and painful sore spot on the sole of my right foot—that if Mamm herself had magically appeared at my side and asked what was up, I might have been totally tongue tied, or told her there was nothing at all the matter. Just now, although I missed her all day and every day, it was for my father that I urgently wished. Somehow I felt sure that if only he would come home, everything would sort itself out, everything would return to normal. Whatever *normal* might be.

Tim trotted along the street, panting and large eyed.

"I say, he's a funny-looking old stick, isn't he? Old Joshua? Mind you, my dad says that it's all rubbish, him selling his soul to the devil. My dad says Joshua was a man ahead of his time—like Newton or Einstein —he'd been working on a flying machine, he was brilliant at maths; my aunt Ruth read about it—"

I was amazed that Tim's father had found time to say all that to his son. Tim went on, portentously, "Hey, listen, guess what I've got! Let's go to your house now—I want to try something."

I was not eager to go back to Harken House, but I did very much want to stay with Tim, who was simple, comfortable, and ordinary—and I could think of no reasonable excuse, so I said, "All right."

Harken House was alertly ready for us, waiting and listening. I had never felt so aware of it. As the weather warmed up, the house, built in the first place, Trudl had told me, from ship's timbers, gave off more and more of its own singular essential smell—old resinous wood, tar, dust, salt, *mystery.* And as the old timbers dried in the heat, they creaked; every now and then you'd catch a snap! like the crack of a distant rifle. Each time I came back to it, I thought the house listened to me more intently, was more silently conscious of my arrival. Perhaps it was getting ready to fall down on me?—like that house in the Dickens story about Little Dorrit, which Mamm had read aloud. Or perhaps it *wanted* something? I remembered a Serbian folk tale I had read about a king's palace which kept falling down until a live princess had been walled up in the foundations. Perhaps Harken House wanted a gift, an offering, a sacrifice?

"Let's go down to the cellar," said Tim.

Joan Aiken

The kitchen was tidy, clean, empty. A tap dripped, the coke shifted in the boiler. Nobody was there. Tim started down the stone stair, I took two or three steps after him. But halfway down, I stuck, overcome with violent reluctance.

"I can't go down just now, Tim."

"Why ever not?"

He had pulled something out of his school bag—a thing shaped like a catapult, a pronged stick. "See this?" he said proudly. "It's a hazel twig, for dowsing. I'm going to hunt for the well. I bet it's in the cellar."

"Why not in the garden?"

"No, I've a kind of feeling—"

"Well, I'm going back upstairs."

"What's up?" Tim stared at me in mild surprise. "I feel sick."

"Why on earth should you feel sick?"

Without waiting for my answer, Tim ran on down, eagerly, into the cellar. I filled a cup with cold water and made my way slowly, on unsteady legs, into the dining room, where I sat down at the long table, holding the cup between my clammy hands. The excuse I gave Tim had not been complete invention. I did feel sick—my head swam, my knees were weak and trembly, as if I had just stepped from a swaying boat onto solid land; my forehead was cold with sweat, and yet my cheeks and ears were burning hot and irritable. Two years ago, when I was coming down with measles, I had felt just like this—wrong in several different ways, wrong from head to foot.

Sick and fearful though I was, an impulse of anger and resistance began to grow up inside me. *Why* should I be bullied in this way—taken over—made to say things I didn't understand, used as somebody else's voice box? Why might I not defend myself? Fight back?

I made myself call up a picture of Joshua Harkin— his strong, watchful face, his piercing eyes—and then silently addressed him: Listen! I didn't come here to speak the words that you put into me. I don't want to do it. I *won't* do it! *I was born in this house!* I have as much right here as you. And I am not your servant— or your daughter. Or your mouthpiece. I can refuse to say the words. I do refuse. Get away from me, Joshua Harkin!

I had never made such an effort before, or done anything needing so much concentration. I was sitting quite still at the table—without moving a muscle —yet I felt *expended,* as if I were engaged in a violent struggle with some strong, indomitable opponent—I could only just breathe, I was screwed up to the last degree of my strength, pushing against something, trying to keep it at arm's length. I remembered the phrase *Vade retro, Satanas*—but no—this thing was in front of me—not behind—

Behind me, I heard somebody clear his throat; a familiar, unobtrusive croak, as well known to me as my brother Joe's whistle, or my sister Anna tunelessly humming "Greensleeves." Next, I could smell extra-strong peppermint, together with an everyday whiff of aromatic pipe tobacco and tweed jacket. I heard the crackle of a newspaper. If the stone wall had not been directly behind me, I would have been quite certain that my father Gerald sat there, absorbed in his morning *Times,* puffing at his curved brown pipe.

But the stone wall *was* behind me, and I felt as if an icicle had been laid on the back of my neck.

Then I heard his voice—Gerald's voice—low, controlled, brittle with anger. He cleared his throat and said, "You simply don't know what you are talking about. Your expectations are completely unreasonable. You are behaving like a stupid, spoiled child."

To whom was he speaking? Not to me, surely? His tone made me cringe. He had never spoken to me in such cold fury. If those words were for me, how could I bear life for another day?

But a second voice answered him, a voice half strangled with sobs.

"It's not true, it isn't true. You did—we did—"

"Nonsense! I never did. We never did. And that's quite enough. I don't want to hear any more on this matter. Not a single word."

A wild, stifled weeping followed: sob after muffled sob.

"Hey—I say, Julia—are you all right up there?" called Tim's startled voice from down below in the cellar.

I made some husky, stammered answer.

"I tell you, I shall have to leave, if this goes on," came Gerald's voice with finality.

I could feel the muscles of my throat vibrating as they pushed out the words.

At the moment when Tim called his question from below, the front door had banged. I heard Trudl's quick loud steps crossing the hall and then come on to the polished floor of the dining room.

"Gerald?" she called eagerly. "Gerald—is that *you*?"

Poor thing—her voice was full of incredulous joy and astonishment.

At the moment when she saw me, Tim arrived from the kitchen, beaming with pride, his face pink and his hair threaded with cobwebs.

"It worked, it really did work! Every single time I walked across one particular bit of the floor, that stick would pull straight down. I couldn't stop it. Come quick and see!"

He flourished his forked hazel twig triumphantly.

Trudl made not the slightest attempt to hide her utter disgust and disappointment.

"Tim Bellyap! What in the world are you doing here? I thought I heard—"

It was nothing uncommon for him to come home with me after school and usually Trudl showed a mild approval, but now she sounded as if it were some outrageous intrusion.

"Were you acting plays? Pretending to be your parents, or something?" she went on in a high, furious voice, looking from one of us to the other. "I could hear you from outside the front door! Well, please don't do it here—find somewhere else for your silly games."

She walked hastily into the kitchen, as if to get away from the sight of us. Tim and I stared at one another, he dreadfully dismayed and crestfallen, while I was paralyzed with a sort of sick dread. The cup on the table in front of me, which had been full of water, was now *empty*. Had I drunk that water? And if so, when? I had no memory of doing so. Or had somebody else drunk it?

Tim slowly lowered the hand holding the hazel

twig. "I—perhaps I'd better go," he mumbled miserably.

I found it impossible to speak; my heart thumped, my mouth was all stuck together as if I had run five hundred yards uphill.

But then we heard Trudl give a despairing cry, almost a shriek, from the kitchen.

"Ach, verdammt! Now the bloody thing has gone out."

It was the kitchen boiler she meant. It had been misbehaving for days past, either cold and sulking, or burning much too fast, heating the water almost to boiling point, roaring up to a terrifying and incandescent heat.

We could hear Trudl furiously rattling with a poker; and then she let out a long, moaning wail, as if everything was just too much for her.

This galvanized us; I jumped up, Tim dropped his school bag, we both ran to the kitchen. We found Trudl crouched in front of the boiler in a pool of ash and cinders. She had opened the door and half lifted out the grate, which, as we could see, was all clogged up with a mass of horrible melted clinker, like toffee that has burned and then gone hard, like black twisted rock with a pearly sheen. And, I knew, if you weren't desperately careful in trying to get the clinker out of the boiler, you brought bits of the grate or lumps of firebrick away too. Trudl had given up in despair, dropped the poker onto a pile of ashes, and was rocking herself back and forth, moaning, "I can't stand it, I can't *stand* it! I hate this horrible house, I hate it, hate it, hate it! I wish it would burn down,

I wish it would fall down, oh, why did I ever, ever come here?"

Ineptly, I tried to pat and comfort her. "Don't, Trudl, don't! Do please stop crying—*please!*"

I had never seen such hysterics in my life before. I couldn't ever remember seeing Mamm weep. If she had shed tears over Gerald, they were all gone when I was only a baby.

"Please, Trudl, look—it doesn't matter about the boiler. Really it doesn't! Don't worry about it. Tim and I will light it for you—we'll clear it out. You come and sit in the dining room."

"I'll put the kettle on for a cup of tea," said Tim practically, and did so.

Trudl gulped and drew a deep breath, dabbing at her eyes with a handkerchief. She did not apologize, but looked at us with resigned irritation, as if we were adults.

"Mamm always says it's a horrible house too," I offered.

Trudl sniffed again and, standing up, walked to the kitchen mirror and studied herself. Her face was pink and shiny and blotched, nose red, hair untidied out of its usual neat gilt coronet.

"Oh, *you*—what can *you* know about it," she muttered harshly.

"Mrs. Butcher says no one ever stays in this house very long—it won't allow them."

"You spend far too much time talking to Mrs. Butcher and that idiotic Wyn."

This was so unfair that I found nothing to say. Tim made some tea, strong as dynamite, and poured Trudl a cup. She sipped it, shuddered, grimaced, and lit a cigarette.

"Okay—thanks—I suppose I had better go and powder my nose."

She clip-clopped away, blowing her nose violently as she went, leaving us to grapple with the boiler.

This, in fact, we quite enjoyed. We found a hammer and chisel in the broom cupboard, and managed to chip away most of the cooled-off clinker without doing too much damage to the grate or the inside of the stove. Tim carried two great pailfuls of clinker, cinder, and coke-dust, and dumped them on the ash heap, while I swept the linoleum in front of the boiler, not very thoroughly. Then, in the cellar, we found kindling and newspapers, relaid the fire, and lit it, Tim doing most of the work. He often lit the fires at home, he said; whereas I was strictly forbidden by my stepfather to have any dealings with fires, or lighting them; children and fires, he said, ought to be kept entirely apart.

Watching the new flames rise biddably behind the replaced grate gave me a warm feeling of solid achievement. I said to Tim, as he clanged the boiler door shut and closed the flue ventilator, "I'll come and see your dowsing trick now. Did it really work so well?"

"Yes, it really did!" he said, his face lighting up. "Just wait till I show you!"

But when we looked for the hazel twig, it was nowhere to be found. Somehow or other it must have got muddled up with the bundle of kindling wood, and burned in the boiler; or that was the only explanation for its disappearance that we could think of.

"Never mind," said Tim at last. "There's lots of hazel bushes in our garden hedge. I'll cut another and bring it tomorrow. See you then, I'd better go now. I say, am I as black as you look? I'd better have a wash before I go."

He did, hastily, in the kitchen sink, then left.

Trudl did not come down again that evening, nor did she make supper for either of us. I found myself a piece of cheese, ate it with bread and marmalade, then went to bed.

I read the echo scene in *The Duchess of Malfi*. By now the poor duchess has been murdered by her wicked brothers, and her widowed husband, walking by her grave, hears an echo which mournfully repeats what he says. Reading this was like an echo, in itself, of another queer thing that had lately been teasing me: things happened to me in patterns, in repetitions. If I dreamed of something at night, of deafness for instance, I was sure to come a reminder of the dream next day, often not once, but two or three times. One night I dreamed—and why should I?—of Gerald's voice saying, "Monteverdi; that is the same name as Greenberg, you know." This meant nothing to me, but next day Miss Sybil told Tim and me something about a composer of music called Monteverdi ("Which means *green hill* in English, you know," she had added); later Tim went off to his music lesson with a book called *Greenberg's Easy Sonatas,* and when I got home that night, Trudl mentioned that she was going off to sing a piece by Monteverdi at her choir practice.

So the echo scene in *The Duchess of Malfi* was no comfort to me.

* *79* *

I felt that I had turned into an echo myself; that like a hollow shell or empty vessel I was passing back sounds and messages that I did not understand.

That night I had a strange dream, of a huge kitchen with black corrugated walls of iron, and ten great copper stoves gleaming against the dark background of the walls, giving off a powerful smell of brewing, hot, salty, and yeasty. A door with a brass lock led out of this room, and my father, Gerald, kneeling with his forehead pressed against the brass lock, was groping over the wall with his hands, as if searching for a secret fastening.

"I'm looking for the way out!" he called. I began passing my own hands over the ridged walls—and woke, with a horrible start, to find myself, not in my bed at all, but standing alone somewhere in the pitch dark, my feet on cold bare boards, my hands touching a plaster wall.

Where in the world was I? Screwing up the courage to move, to feel about, to discover where I had got to, was one of the worst, most difficult things I had ever done. But in the end I did move my hands—found a door frame—and then, groping up and down, felt the four wooden steps, the four steps that led down into Gerald's study, which I must have crossed while still asleep. Turning round I made my way back, inching along, to my own room, and climbed in among the cold tangled sheets. How long had I been out of bed? Ten minutes? Half an hour?

It was a long, chilly time before I went back to sleep.

Chapter Six

THE WEATHER had suddenly turned hot. Even at breakfast next morning it was close and sultry.

Trudl was pale, and said little, but she seemed to have forgotten yesterday's outburst; she was frowning over a headline in the paper which said that the Germans who lived in the part of Czechoslovakia called the Sudetenland were asking for autonomy.

"What's autonomy?" I asked, drinking the cocoa which, quite contrary to habit, she had made for me. Perhaps it was intended as an apology.

"Autonomy? Oh—self-government, wanting to rule themselves, not being ruled over by the Czech government. Of course it would really mean Germany taking over that area. And if they do take it, then Poland will take a piece of Czechoslovakia— Hungary will take a piece—they are like vultures snatching at a carcass—oh, it is disgusting!"

"But, *can* countries just take pieces of other countries?"

"Germany took Austria," she said bitterly. "All my friends and family are being ruled by Germans now."

I went slowly off to school with a feeling that the whole world was breaking up into bits like lava in a volcano—nations were melting and falling apart, people were being separated from one another; and I myself belonged nowhere, didn't belong to myself any longer; other people's voices gushed out of my mouth; I felt as if my own mind were being pushed out of joint, thrust aside, bent, first one way, then another, by forces I could not understand.

How—how in the world—could *Gerald's and Trudl's* voices have come bursting out of my mouth?

I had thought about it for hours in the night. Was it that some of their words were trapped in the house, preserved forever in some incomprehensible way— perhaps by the violence with which they had first been spoken? Was *that* what the house did? Caught sounds, and kept them suspended, like flies in webs, like plums in syrup? Could it have been something Joshua Harkin did that first started this process?

I wondered what answers Mamm would give to these questions. In my mind I could hear her clear voice. *"Don't* pick your nose. *Do* pull your shoulders back. Always squeeze woollen things when you wash them, don't wring. Think for yourself. Decide for yourself." Mamm, in a reassuring way, by suggesting to me what I ought to do, managed to give me a firm idea of myself, and what I ought to *be*. Like a map, she defined boundaries on a flat surface. But what she would make of what was happening to me now—not flat at all, but three dimensional, four dimensional, other people's voices cascading out of me like oil gushers—I could not possibly imagine.

And what about Gerald? What would *he* think?

"I've brought another twig," said Tim hopefully, before our first lesson at school—English with Miss Madge— "Can I come round to your house this afternoon and try it?"

Tim was like a bulldog; once he got an idea he hung on to it forever.

"Better not, if Trudl is there," I warned him. "Let's wait and see."

His face fell. But I couldn't pay much attention to Tim, I was filled with horrible misgiving, scared that the voices might gush out of me at school, and what would I do *then*? Excuse myself, pretend to sneeze, rush to the toilet? Pretend nothing had happened? Something of the kind *had* happened once before, I remembered, when Miss Lucy had been reading Scripture; and there were the times at the library and down on the Salts; just being away from the house itself was no protection.

Would I be at the mercy of these voices forever? For the rest of my life?

Lessons with Miss Madge were always enjoyable because she could be led to talk about all kinds of things. Just now she was talking about Bernard Shaw's play *St. Joan*, and reading aloud bits from it.

"Of course many people nowadays would say that

Joan was mad, schizophrenic," she said. "But Shaw doesn't take that view."

"I thought schizophrenic meant that you had a split personality, were two different people," said Tim.

"No, Tim, it means that what you think in your mind doesn't connect with your behavior, what you do."

Lots of people are like *that,* I thought. Things are going on in my mind all the time that don't have any connection with what I actually do.

"But Shaw believes in Joan's voices, just as she did," Miss Madge went on. "You can tell that because he makes the wind change and the hens start laying eggs as soon as she is given her way. The play is about how different people make use of Joan for their own purposes."

"Do *you* believe in Joan's voices, Miss Madge?" said Tim.

Miss Madge turned a little pink. "Well, Tim, I think that many of us have our own voices, like Joan," she answered cautiously after a moment. "As you grow older, you notice them more."

More? I thought. Oh, no, no! I want them to stop. I don't want any more.

"Sometimes a person and a time can come together," Miss Madge was saying. "One individual seems to speak with the voice of a whole nation. As Joan did."

"Like Hitler?" I suggested.

She frowned.

"Hitler is an example of how such a thing can

work for evil as well as for good. A whole people can pick up some sick, wrong idea, just like an infection."

"So the voices can be bad as well as good?"

"Now, I think we have talked about voices enough," said Miss Madge. Later in the lesson she mentioned a couple of Gerald's plays, *Christmas at Cumae* and *The Truth Sayer*. She said the people in them always started by cheating and betraying each other, then spent the rest of the play trying to make amends.

"Usually without success," she said, smiling faintly, and added something about redemption which I didn't understand. She asked if I had read his plays, and I was obliged to admit that, though I had started two or three, I had stuck in them. Nothing seemed to happen, the characters just spent the play arguing. Whereas, in *The Duchess of Malfi*—which, for lack of other reading, I had now finished—there was plenty of action, the characters never stopped doing hateful things to one another, swindling, plotting, lying, and murdering. Just reading the play made me feel like a secret agent.

I said something about it to Miss Madge and she cried out in horror.

"Good heavens, child, where in the world did you find *that*—first *Dr. Faustus* and now Webster—of all the disgusting, unsuitable—"

Quickly, to distract her, because I saw she was likely to lend me a whole armful of *John and Mary* readers, I asked her about Joshua Harkin.

"What do you think was the real story, Miss Madge?"

"Oh, my dear! Are you still on about him? Can't

you children find better things to occupy your minds?"

"We want to find out about him," said Tim.

"He's interesting," I said.

"Well, if you want my opinion," said Miss Madge, "I think he was misjudged. *I* don't believe he meant to hurt his son-in-law. Probably the boy would have died in any case, traveling from France when he was ill. And the neighbors all agreed that Joshua had been fond of Ralph. Of course Joshua must have felt horribly let down by his daughter. Why don't you try writing a play about him?" she said to me.

"*I? A play?*" I was dumbfounded. What an idea! Such a thing would never have occurred to me. "But how would it end?"

"Well, that would be up to you, wouldn't it?" she said, smiling. "Oh, dear, there's twelve o'clock striking, and we've done hardly any work."

AFTER SCHOOL that evening Tim came round to Harken House and waited outside in the street while I checked to see if Trudl was in. But she was not. She disappeared on her bicycle sometimes for hours together; I never knew where.

I beckoned Tim in, and we went down to the cellar. Today I had no feeling of apprehension; the house seemed clear and empty. But, to our great disappointment, the new hazel twig that Tim had brought would not perform for him. Although he paced diligently to and fro, back and forth, his carefully cut dowsing-stick refused to make any signal. At last he flung it down in disgust and said that he must go; his aunt Ruth was coming to supper.

After he had gone I picked up the twig and, out of curiosity, held it as he had done, the leg of the Y pointing forward, and my thumbs pointing backward.

I began to walk about, over the cellar floor.

Almost at once, the twig gave a vicious tug, and leapt out of my hands. I gasped—then, with my heart beating thunderously, picked it up and tried again. The same thing happened. And Patty's voice burst out of me with the force of a fire hydrant.

"I'd *die* to get away from you—do you know that? I would truly sooner die than stay in this house with you!"

And Joshua's voice, answering: "Girl, girl, can't you believe me? Try to believe that we might still make a life together."

"No!" she cried. "No, never, never! I shall hate you to the end of my life!"

"Hallo-allo-allo-ee?" called a voice from upstairs. "Anybody home? Jule? Are you down there? In the *cellar*? Whatever are you doing down *there*?"

I went slowly up and found Wyn in the kitchen, adjusting her hair in the glass, humming one of her doleful songs.

"Poor little Willie, he's deaf and he's dumb,
Poor little Willie's insane,
Poor little Willie has only one leg,
What a shame, what a shame, what a
    shame. . . ."

"What have you been up to?" she said, looking at me slant eyed.

* *87* *

Just then I didn't think I could stand the company of Wyn.

"I've got to go back to school," I mumbled. "Something—a book—I left behind. Can't stop—I need it for my homework."

And I raced out of the house, down the hill, and up Chapel Passage. By now, I knew, the Norns would have gone; they had a house in Ackenden, seven miles away. The little building would be empty and locked up. But by now I knew where the key was kept —under one of the hydrangea tubs—and I had often gone back there after school when I could not face the emptiness of Harken House on my own.

Cautiously—after listening at the keyhole to make sure nobody was inside, moving about—I let myself in. Perhaps under the influence of the characters in *The Duchess of Malfi* I was becoming a furtive, secretive character myself. I had to keep so many things hidden away inside me—for who would listen, who would believe?

No sound came, so I went in, made myself comfortable at Miss Sybil's desk, and looked over her notes and jottings. I read a pile of the younger children's compositions, and her comments on them, inspected the model village they had made from matchsticks and clay, studied the marks that Miss Lucy had given me for an essay on Henry VIII.

He was a bad father, because he sent his children away, I had written, and she had noted in red ink, *This was customary in Tudor times. Other things more important. Why Wolsey not mentioned?*

I found a new *John and Mary* reader, and read it, with a sort of gloating contempt. Then I investigated the little closet where the Norns hung their coats and kept tea and biscuits. Sadly, the tin held only two biscuits; to take one would be too noticeable. Along-side the biscuit tin on its shelf was a brown paper parcel with a label: RICE FLAKES PRODUCTS. Perhaps it held our airplanes? Longing to look inside, I lifted and shook it; it rattled, interestingly. But there was no possible way of undoing it without detection, so, re-gretfully, I put it back. By now Wyn would have gone home, I judged; she never liked being in Harken House by herself. I locked up, carefully replaced the key in its hiding place, and trudged slowly home-ward.

Mercifully, Trudl had come back, and was wheel-ing her bicycle through the kitchen to the garden shed.

She made no allusion to where she had been, but said, "There's another postcard for you. Came by the afternoon post."

This one was postmarked Évian, and showed an extravagant fairy-tale castle perched on a crag. *Fran-kenstein lived here with the Prisoner of Zenda. Both their toothbrushes are on show,* Gerald had written. *Hope you are learning a lot. Love, G.*

"It's a lovely castle," I said, disappointed. "But I wish he'd write more."

"Your father," said Trudl, "prefers buildings to people. He prefers trees to buildings, and rivers to trees. And he prefers the ocean to everything else." In her voice there was a kind of despairing fury. She walked away into the kitchen and I heard a sizzle as she dropped two herrings into the frying pan.

There are *too many* voices in this house, I thought

unhappily. Too many angry voices, all asking to be
heard.

Trudl went out again immediately after supper,
and I went to bed by daylight. First I tried to bring my
accounts up to date in the little book that Mamm had
given me. But I had fallen hopelessly behind; the
amount of money left in my purse bore no relation at
all to the sums I had written down in the book. After
shedding some despairing tears over it, I read *Hans
Brinker* for perhaps the seventh time. None of Gerald's books on the study shelves was any use to me. I
had looked them over and over. Some were in French
or German, some in Spanish or Italian; and those that
were in English were in verse of a very modern kind,
or they were not stories but long discussions about
literary or philosophical matters, miles beyond my
mental reach. *The Dynamics of Possession,* one was
called. What was *that* about? I had no idea.

When at last I fell asleep I dreamed that I had got
up and dressed and gone out to follow Trudl and see
where she went in the evenings. Up cobbled Harbor
Hill I followed her, round the corner into South
Street, and so into Church Square and across the
churchyard. But there I banged my knee on a grave-
stone and woke myself.

With a familiar feeling of dread I found that I was
out of bed, upright, standing in the dark, I could not
tell where. But this time, after a moment or two, I was
able to place myself by the smell around me—a familiar smell of scented soap, and gas leaking, and old
tarnished copper. I really had given my knee a bang. I
felt about at knee level and found the enamel side of
the bath, and the rough toweling bathmat that hung

over it. I was in the bathroom; thank heaven it was no worse than that.

But after I had gone back to bed I lay in the dark for a long time, quaking, wondering where I might wander next. Perhaps I had better give up getting undressed when I went to bed?

And again I remembered that cold, damp touch on my hand.

NEXT DAY, with ceremony, Miss Sybil handed Tim and me our Frog planes. She explained carefully that no favoritism was involved; the little ones were going to receive a cardboard model town, also obtained by box tops from Rice Flakes.

The planes were beautiful, made of oiled silk over wooden frames, light and strong, with clockwork propellers. We longed to try them at once, but there was no sufficiently large open space near the school, so we had to wait. After school we took them down on to the Town Salts.

("Let's hope that will keep their little heads from getting so stuffed up with ghosts and nonsense," I heard Miss Sybil say to Miss Lucy as we left.)

The planes performed magnificently, taking long, airy curving flights over the grass. Tim's landed with more grace, but mine flew farther, floating on gallantly for astonishing distances.

Without in the least having intended to, I found myself telling Tim that his hazel twig had worked for me, and he became excited all over again.

"I told Aunt Ruth about it last night and she was ever so interested—she's the secretary of the Dune

Historical Society. So—if it works for you—she said she'd like to come and see, sometime—"

"Oh, I don't think Trudl would want that," I said hastily. "We'll have to see."

But Tim hurried off homeward full of plans—perhaps his aunt Ruth could get the Historical Society interested in coming to look for the well. "There might be treasure in it," he said hopefully. "People often did hide treasure in wells."

THE NEXT WEEKEND was a bank holiday. Tim was going with his parents to an uncle in Rochester on Saturday, but on Friday, as there was no school, he and I walked down to the beach. The weather was still very hot. Trudl was working hard on the last part of her translation and couldn't come, but gave us a bottle of lemonade and a shilling to buy food. With it we bought Lyons twopenny fruit pies, three apiece, apple, apricot, and strawberry.

We spent the morning swimming in the warm shallow sea—Tim could really swim, I walked about on my hands in the water and pretended I was swimming; then looked for shells, then lay on our stomachs and ate our fruit pies and talked about Joshua Harkin.

"He wrote a big book on mathematics," Tim said. "Aunt Ruth has seen it in the county museum. It's all about infinity; things like that. I don't believe he was a wizard at all. Just an ordinary person—a kind of writer, maybe, like your dad."

Perhaps Joshua *was* rather like Gerald, I thought in surprise; too busy working on his book to have any time for other people. If ever *I* had children, I resolved, I would spend all my spare time teaching them, or taking them on outings.

"They probably wouldn't thank you," Tim commented when I told him this. "Who wants to have parents around bothering all the time? Your children would probably rather go off on their own."

You always want what you haven't got, I thought.

When we started the long walk home, our backs felt rather warm and itchy. And by the time we reached Harken House, they were bright scarlet and fiercely sore.

Trudl, just setting off with a parcel for the post office when we arrived, gave us both a scolding.

"*Stupid* children—why couldn't you have more *sense*? Lying in the hot sun all day—what *do* you expect? I'll have to get some sunburn stuff—there is none in the house."

She came back with a tube of oily yellow goo called citronella, which smelled very strong but didn't seem to help the pain. Tim walked slowly off toward his home, carrying his shirt over his arm, and I went and lay on my stomach on the sitting-room floor and looked at an old bound volume of *Punch* from 1890 which I had found in the cupboard under the stairs. The jokes in it seemed very laborious and long-winded, and I didn't understand the political cartoons, but I liked the drawings. By and by Trudl put her head round the door to say that she was going to choir practice and would be back late; I was to have my supper and go to bed.

"You'd better lie on *top* of your bed—it won't matter as it's so hot. And I don't want that stuff all over the sheets. If you can't sleep, take an aspirin—I've left the bottle out in the bathroom."

Her step clipped down the stair and I heard the slam of the front door.

Though I was not in the least hungry I went down to see what she had left me for supper. Under a saucepan lid there were three sardines and some slices of bread-and-butter. I ate them standing in the kitchen. Sitting in a chair was too uncomfortable, because I daren't lean back. While eating, I read a story in an old newspaper left by Mrs. Butcher about the Monsters of the Marsh. The Monsters turned out to be, rather disappointingly, two fifteen-year-old boys who had gone round to isolated marshland farms, finding and stealing people's little hoards of savings. Up to now they had been seen at a distance but never caught. They seemed very clever at finding money, no matter how ingeniously it had been hidden away. "DO put your savings in the bank!" the newspaper was urging its readers. "DON'T risk the chance of these young scoundrels finding and making off with your nest egg!"

I wondered if the Marsh Monsters ever ventured into Dune. But people living in a town would be more likely to have their money in the bank, because the bank was so much closer, just along the High Street; so thieves wouldn't expect to find cash and jewelry secreted in bread bins or coal scuttles. But still, might they not have heard the story of Joshua Harkin's supposed hoard of treasure at the bottom of the well—if there *was* a well? Then I scolded myself for childish thoughts. Joshua Harkin had been dead for hundreds of years. Why should anybody search for his treasure now? I was really just thinking these things to distract myself from the pain of my back, which felt as if it had been scalded with boiling oil.

I tried to rub on some more citronella, but it was very difficult. Leaving my supper plate unwashed, I went upstairs to the bathroom and took an aspirin; as that seemed to make no difference to the agony, I took a couple more.

I tried lying on my bed, but the blankets and sheets quickly became tangled and wrinkled under me and were too hot and uncomfortable to be borne, so I wandered downstairs again to the sitting room and spread Mrs. Butcher's paper, sheet by sheet, all over the floor, to prevent my smearing citronella on the rugs. HITLER THREATENS SUDETENLAND, said a big headline under my right elbow. Trudl's little radio had been left on the sitting-room window-sill; I switched it on and Hitler's voice poured out— the radio was tuned in to a German station—bawling out some angry, threatening message, while a huge crowd in the background bayed out its approval and delight. Shivering, I cut off the grim sound. What I longed for was a bit of music—I had never been de-prived of it for so long, at home music was always being played—but I did not like to change Trudl's wavelength.

Stretching out on the sheets of newspaper, I tried to sleep.

The areas of me that were not burning with pain now became very cold. I was obliged to cover my legs and arms with towels, which, as I shifted about in misery, kept falling off. Oh, how I longed for Mamm. Surely she would have found something better than citronella to put on my raging back? Perhaps when Trudl came back she would think of some other remedy. . . .

It took ages for me to get off to sleep, because each time, just as I was growing drowsy, my own whimpering woke me again. But at last I began to dream about some cottage garden where I was watering the plants; and the black dog kept getting in my way, nearly tripping me as I plodded back and forth, carrying a heavy galvanized iron watering-can.

"You will need more water than that," said a voice. "You will have to go to the well. Be sure the Marsh Monsters don't follow you. Tell the dog to be quiet."

I had seen the well, ringed by a brick coping, with a little roof over it, supported on two posts, and a cone-shaped bucket on a chain. I told the dog not to bark, and started hunting, but now dark had fallen and the well was nowhere in view.

"Light a bonfire," said the voice—Gerald's?— "then you'll be able to see where to hang your bucket."

The matches kept slipping like threads between my fingers, and would not strike. I was almost crying with frustration and the pain from my back; in the end I flung the whole box on the ground, shouting, "*Damn* the stupid matches! I'll light a wax taper at the boiler."

My own shout woke me. A lot of little things had fallen on my feet, and when I stooped to feel them (as on the two previous occasions, I found myself standing somewhere in the dark) I could feel tiny sticks that must be matches. After a moment or two I found the box and was able to strike a light.

By its tiny glimmer I could then see, with a feeling of sick shock, that I was in the cellar.

The flame burned down to my fingers and went out, but now I was able to find the switch and turn on the light. Thank heaven for electricity! I had been standing by the piles of coke and kindling and packets of fire lighters; matches were sprinkled around me over the stone-flagged floor.

Please, please, *don't* let this be happening, I prayed, as I knelt to pick them up, scraping my finger-tips on the gritty floor-surface. Oh, what in the world would Mamm say to *this*?

I took the roughly refilled matchbox back to the kitchen and put it on the shelf by the sink where it was normally kept. Then I washed my sardine plate, which I had forgotten earlier, with tears running down my cheeks, rubbing it again and again to get rid of the fishy smell. There Trudl found me when she came in.

"What in the name of goodness do you think you are doing, up at this hour?" she scolded. "It's after midnight!" and then, seeing, I suppose, the state I was in, she said she was going to fetch Dr. Coulthard, who lived just up at the top of the hill. He arrived five minutes later and said I wouldn't remember him (he was right) but that he had brought me into the world, and what was all this carry-on for a simple case of sunburn?—though a very nasty one, he must admit, people with red hair always got it worst. Perhaps that would teach me not to lie for hours in the hot sun.

He sent me up to bed, laid wet bandages all over

my back, and gave me a disgusting dose of something which sent me straight to sleep and left me sleeping for about thirteen hours. During that time I dreamed a tremendous amount, but hazy, tangled dreams, nothing to remember and hang on to after waking. When I did wake, at around teatime on Saturday, the pain in my back was much milder, and Trudl was there with a big mug of homemade lemonade and a box of dominoes borrowed from the doctor, whose children were all grown up.

The rest of the weekend I spent in a state of convalescence, wearing an old angora jumper of Trudl's, since even the lightest of my Aertex shirts was too rough and painful on my skin.

It was a big relief when school started again on Tuesday.

Nothing happened for ten days, except that Mamm's little clock developed a habit of clearing its throat, as if the alarm were about to sound off, although I hadn't wound the alarm key. This little noise always woke me. My sleep was light and jumpy at this time; every night before I went to bed I laid out a series of obstacles, bags and cases taken from the box room, between my bed and the door, so that if I walked in my sleep, I might trip over them and wake myself up.

Why hadn't I told Dr. Coulthard about the sleepwalking?

I was too embarrassed.

Then, one morning at breakfast, it was plain that something had upset Trudl dreadfully. Her face was all blotched and shiny, from tears I supposed, her hands shook so that she could hardly hold her coffee cup.

"Is there bad news about Czechoslovakia?" I ventured timidly—really meaning, What is the matter? but not daring to come straight out with that.

"No!" Trudl snapped and, without explanation, picked up her cup and carried it into the kitchen. I gulped down my egg in haste and took my own plate and cup to the sink. Trudl was standing motionless, staring out at the fringe of mint on the area wall. She ignored me as I washed my dishes, but I thought I had seen her swiftly thrust a piece of paper into her skirt pocket as I came in. It could have been the grayish writing paper generally used by Gerald, with his black scratchy writing on it. Was it a letter from him? If so, what could he have said in it, to distress her so terribly?

Burning with unsatisfied curiosity, I gathered my things together and set off slowly toward school. At lunchtime, when I came back, Mrs. Butcher was there and supplied me with a plate of salad. Trudl was nowhere about, and when I asked where she was, Mrs. Butcher shook her head and shrugged. She, too, seemed unusually silent and glum, only muttering something about that there Hitler turning the whole world topsy turvy as she gave me a banana for dessert.

In the afternoon there was to be a school outing, of a sort; Miss Lucy proposed to take Tim and me and half a dozen of the larger "smaller ones" to the town museum. At half past two, under a heavy, hot gray sky like a trash-can lid, we all walked round to the Old Guildhall, two by two, with Miss Lucy bringing up the rear.

"It's frightfully boring," Tim muttered to me. "I've been there twice before."

There were four rooms, containing a mixed accumulation of odds and ends: a wasps' nest, stuffed birds, geological specimens, dried snakes, and a relief model, made in plaster painted green and brown, of Dune and the surrounding countryside. There were also seashells and tanks of marine life, and examples of the local trees and flowers. And there was a large beautiful doll's house (which was all the little ones wished to look at) and various agricultural implements, wooden plows, tools, shepherd's crooks and smocks, yokes and pails, milking stools and butter pats.

Every object had the dry, dusty leathery smell that is so peculiar to small museums. And the building itself was stuffy and dark—becoming darker, too, all the time, for the sky was clouding up, piles of lumpy soot-black cumulus were massing in great pointed mountains. Dune is famed for its thunderstorms, but it was plain that this one was going to be extraspecial.

"Oh, my gracious!" exclaimed Miss Lucy, glancing out through one of the narrow pointed windows. "I think we had best cut short our visit; the museum garden had better wait for another day. We must scurry—I fear we should have brought rainwear along with us—make haste, children!"

Nobody minded missing the museum garden, which was merely a flagged yard, in which stone pots contained plants that Shakespeare had mentioned. But I would have liked to linger a bit longer in the last small room, which had an exhibition of oil paintings on its walls.

"Who *did* them?" I asked, as Miss Lucy rushed us past the pictures.

"Some local man—they look rather *modern,*" she said with disapproval. As we scuffled by, the smaller children bumping and squeaking ahead of us, I caught a glimpse of copper tubes against gray-and-black verticals, of a man kneeling with his arms extended, of a small shapeless building crumbling under a pitiless storm, of a black dog. . . .

Why did those images seem so queerly familiar? As we filed in haste through the narrow glass doors I realized that it was because the pictures—or several of them, at any rate—were like illustrations of my own dreams, the dreams I had been having since I came to Dune. The kitchen with its copper brewing vats, the house in the storm, the black dog, Gerald in an attitude of prayer—of course they were familiar! I thought I had invented them myself. But perhaps I had picked them out of the air from somebody else?

"What is the painter's name?" I asked Tim in a stunned voice.

"Not sure. Something short—Baker—Thatcher? my aunt Ruth knows him—*blimey!*" He gasped. "Look!"

A lurid blue-white bayonet of lightning had sliced straight across the piled-up murky background of cloud.

"Run, children!" shrilled Miss Lucy, and we all broke into a frantic gallop. Of course it was quite hopeless. As a tremendous clap of thunder exploded overhead, the rain came down, not in single drops, but in jugfuls, in pailfuls, in barrels of water that

roared in a solid mass from the heavens. After a dozen yards all of us were completely drenched.

"You can't go back to school like that!" gasped Miss Lucy as we careered across Church Square. "You must each of you go straight to your own homes and put on dry clothes immediately. And you need not come back to school today."

"What about me?" from Tim, grinning at her through the streaks of sopping mouse-colored hair that hung over his forehead.

"I will drive you home, my dear boy; I shall have to go home and change myself, and I can drop you on the way," Miss Lucy told him.

I was rather relieved to hear that, for I had been afraid Miss Lucy might suggest his coming round to dry off at Harken House; I did not think Trudl would want him there if she were still as upset as she had been before school. Also I had plans of my own.

"Hullo?" I called, when I burst through the front door. "Hullo, is anybody there?" but I received no answer. The house felt empty. I went into the kitchen, where Trudl had stood looking out at the mint. There I combed expertly through the wastebasket and trash can, but found no trace of the letter I thought I had seen in her hand.

Hurrying up the stairs to her workroom—empty, likewise—I searched her work table, its drawer, and the wastebasket. Nothing there. Then I tried her bedroom, the door of which stood open. It was extremely untidy—clothes were hanging half pulled out of drawers, the bed was unmade, powder spilled from a box onto the chest-of-drawers top, half a dozen cigarette stubs were squashed in the saucer of a dirty

coffee cup. I thought how shocked Mamm would be—
and then thought, also, how utterly horrified she
would be to see *me*, prying through other people's
belongings in this underhand way. But I went on doing it, urgently, feverishly. I rummaged under the
pillow, in drawers, in pockets, boxes, even between
the pages of books.

But no, nothing.

Then, for some reason, it occurred to me to go and
hunt on Gerald's own desk, which, ever since I came
to the house, had remained tidy, unaltered, gathering
dust, in the first of the two rooms that made up his
study, with the chair pushed in, orderly and imper-
sonal.

An engagement diary lay on the desktop, with the
last marked date in it several weeks before my own
arrival. I flipped over the pages. Nothing was tucked
between them. A mug held pencils and pens. The
basket was empty. A folder held letters—business
ones mostly, typed, with printed headings. Nothing
there. A little miniature Japanese chest-of-drawers,
made from inlaid wood and mother-of-pearl, stood at
the back of the desk. It contained notes and smaller
papers, I knew; I had poked through its contents
once, during some of those long idle hours when I was
alone in the house. The top drawer held letters from
Trudl, several years old, and all in German. *"Liebstes
Herz,"* they began. The middle drawer held letters
from somebody I had never heard of who signed himself "Bob" and illustrated the text with little drawings. The bottom one had been empty before—
but—*aha!*

It *was* a letter from Gerald, dated this week, from Évian.

My dear Trudl, it began, *your constant stream of childish, whining expostulations leaves me no choice and can no longer be borne. All I can tell you is, now, finally, once and for all, that I am never coming back to you. Ours was intended for a purely business arrangement—as you well knew—and you must understand that is over now and for good. You may stay in the house for the rest of the summer, until Julia has finished her term; then I plan to put the house up for sale, so you will have to make other plans. By the way, I hear from people in Dune who seem very concerned (I will not mention their names lest I lay them open to your childish spite and hostility) that you have been taking very poor care of the child, go out to classes every evening, are hardly ever in the house, and have left her to her own devices often for days together. I should have thought that simple gratitude might have urged you to behave a little better to the poor child. But that, apparently, would be too much to hope.*

I leave Évian tomorrow, without a forwarding address, so it is no use your writing any more letters to me. G.

All the breath drained out of me as I read this letter, the blood sank from my heart, and I found it almost impossible to fill up my lungs again—I had to gasp and gasp unavailingly, like a person who has breathed in poison gas. I felt weak and sick, as if the deadly blow had been dealt to me, not to Trudl. What must she have *felt*! No wonder she had been so shocked and silent at breakfast, so trembling and red-eyed.

All of a sudden I sincerely hated my father. How could he be so coldly, deliberately unkind, so horrible to poor harmless pink-cheeked Trudl? She was looking after his house, she was looking after me (not very well, but never mind that)—and she couldn't even answer back since he had gone without leaving an address. You pig, you pig, you utter pig, I shouted at him in my mind. I don't care if I never set eyes on you again.

With all my heart I longed for Mamm to come and set matters right—tell Trudl that she'd be better off without Gerald (who would never, really, care for anything but his plays)—tell me that my own queer state was pure imagination, or, anyway, not important, and would stop as soon as I was safely back at home.

But I knew very well that Mamm, like Gerald, would never come to this house again.

I am on a desert island along with a lot of ghosts, I thought, and walked on stiff aching legs through to my own bedroom, where I crumpled up and dropped on the bed, still in my soaking-wet school clothes. Without making any effort to take them off I huddled, shivering, shaken, and battered by a terrible fit of tears; I hiccupped, sobbed, and gasped; for whom I was weeping I hardly knew; for myself, perhaps, for Trudl, for Joshua, for Patty; for the house itself, soon to be deserted again. But perhaps that was what the house liked best, what it preferred—to be left empty, uninhabited, to hold its own griefs in its own heart?

Trudl came through and found me there. She had

not expected me at all—holding a bunch of luggage
labels, she walked straight through into the boxroom
and emerged carrying a small suitcase. Then she saw
me and dropped the bag with a quick sharp breath. I
still held Gerald's letter clutched in my hand. She saw
that, too, instantly.

"So!" said Trudl, on a long, harsh note. "So! You
prying, sneaking little beast! I believe that you deserve to have such a father—that is all I can say!"

She picked up the bag and walked out of the
room. I heard her hasty steps cross the study and
mount the four stairs.

"Trudl!" I called, but my voice came in a croak
and was, anyway, drowned by a huge clap of thunder
—for the storm was still raging, unabated; I could
hear rain lash down on the flat roof and splatter
against the wide glass pane of the studio window.
Whether Trudl heard my voice or not, she made no
answer.

I fell back on my pillow again and went on help-
lessly crying. In the end, I suppose, I must have cried
myself to sleep, for I began to dream. I dreamed of
Joshua with his dog. He was trying on a pair of wings,
like Icarus; they were made of oiled silk and attached
to his chest by means of crisscross straps. The big
black dog sat by him and whined. We were up on a
stone parapet with a big drop beyond.

"It's the well," Joshua said to me, but I could see
that he was wrong. It was not the well, it was the town
wall. "Now, Bellman, you must go," Joshua said to the
dog, who whined again. "Run along—under the arch
there—go! You can't come with me this time. Go! Go
seek! Go seek!" He waved his arm impatiently toward

RETURN TO HARKEN HOUSE

a low arch in the wall, trying to make the dog leave
him, but it was miserably unwilling to do so. "*You* will
have to take Bellman," Joshua told me.

"The dog? I? Why should I? I don't like dogs. Why
should I?"

"Because you are my daughter and must do as I
say." His tone was inflexible.

He turned away and I could no longer see him.
The dream changed, and I was walking along a flat
path across the marsh, bounded by a ditch on each
side. The dog trotted at my side, occasionally questing
a little way ahead, whining pitifully as if he still
searched for his master.

Then, far ahead, I began to see familiar roofs, set
among well-known trees. When I had walked a little
farther, I recognized the roofs and trees of home and
could—with a leap of the heart—see the figure of
Mamm herself come out and stand shading her eyes,
looking in my direction.

She will be dreadfully cross about Bellman, I
thought. And puzzled too! She will wonder where in
the world I found him and what in the world we are
going to do with him. She doesn't like dogs a bit.

The dream changed again, though, and I did not
see how Mamm dealt with the dog; now I was alone,
in the dark, at the bottom of a deep well, with nobody
near; only, and this was strange, I could still hear the
dog whine and whimper.

After that I realized that my eyes were open, wide
open, staring into blackness; I could hear the whimpering still, but it came from myself. I was standing on
a rough, uneven surface, in the pitch dark, and all I
could guess of my whereabouts was that it must be

out of doors, for the air felt bitterly cold, occasional drops of rain stung my face, and a sharp wind made me shiver.

I cleared my throat and called, "Please—help! Where am I? Can anyone hear me? Trudl? Are you there? Oh, please, please help me, somebody!"

Nobody answered. But a moment later the place was lit by a great wispy violet-colored network of lightning—like a cobweb across the sky—which showed me, to my stunned horror, that I was standing on the parapet wall of the cliff gardens, with the steeply sloping cliff and the outer ring road just below me. Next moment the sky went black again, black as velvet, and, with the crash of thunder that followed, I lost my unsteady footing, overbalanced, toppled off the wall, and rolled, over and over, down the cliff.

I felt a sharp series of pains and bumps—from stones, sticks, thorns, brambles, stubs of brushwood—then a much worse pain as my head hit some hard object—then nothing at all.

Chapter Seven

WHEN I WOKE AGAIN it was daylight, I was in my own bed, and Mrs. Butcher was bringing me a cup of something. Behind her was Dr. Coulthard.

"Well, young woman! Never a dull moment with you! You gave poor Constable Peasmarsh a fright, I can tell you," he boomed at me in his jovial extraloud voice. "Sleepwalking in the cliff gardens, what next? Rolling down into the road. Lucky there wasn't any traffic around at that time of night, eh?"

"What time of night was it?" I asked faintly.

"What time? Oh, about four in the morning. Make a habit of this sleepwalking, do you, eh?"

"Never before I came here—but how did you

know I was sleepwalking?" I asked confusedly, as he sat down on the bed and felt my bandaged head. It was tender and I winced at his touch.

"Sore, is it? I'm not surprised. You got a bit of concussion there, old lady—no more than you deserve either. How do we know—because old Canon Teape saw you, out of his bedroom window (he's a wakeful old fellow, spends half the night pottering around looking through night glasses) he saw you under the streetlight at the corner of the High Street, gliding along like Lady MacB. So he telephoned the police, and young Peasmarsh went out hunting for you. Looked all over, finally found you in a heap at the bottom of the cliff. Fine goings-on! So then they fetched me out."

"Here, drink that," said Mrs. Butcher when the doctor had looked me over, announced that there was nothing wrong that a day in bed wouldn't put right, and gone humming away across the study and down the stairs. She handed me the cup. It was beef tea, lukewarm and very disgusting, but I was thirsty and drank it.

"Where's Trudl?" I asked then. Mrs. Butcher shook her head slowly, impressively.

"Would you believe it? Gone off to Paris."

"To *Paris*?" I was thunderstruck. "Why?"

"Seems she heard her brother and a friend of his might have a chance to come away out of Austria, if she could get over to Paris and find somebody to answer for 'em," said Mrs. Butcher. "Left me a note and off she went on the seven o'clock. Never even knew you were missing." She shook her head and pursed her lips. "I don't know, I'm sure. Fair amazed I

was, when I got here and found the police and Dr.
Coal-tarred. They sent round to fetch me when they
found she wasn't in."

"Who's—who's—" Who is going to look after me, I
wanted to ask, but felt it sounded childish and whining. Mrs. Butcher said, however, "Wyn or me'll keep
an eye on you till your brother gets here."

"My brother? Is *he* coming?" My heart lifted won-
derfully. Dear, dear Joe—so capable and cheerful—I
felt sure that he would solve every problem right
away.

"Dr. Coulthard said 'e'd sent a telegram to your
mum. And she phoned 'im."

"Oh, goodness—she'll be so worried."

"No, the doctor told 'er you was all right," said
Mrs. Butcher robustly. "So jest you lay still and don't
bother. Here's a comic to look at. And Wyn'll be along
by and by when she's finished round at Mrs.
Spearpoint's."

During the morning, Miss Sybil dropped in to
see me.

"My dear child! What an upset! And I am so very
sorry to hear about your stepmother having gone off
in that unexpected way. I suppose her leaving like
that—so suddenly—was what upset you?"

It seemed too complicated to explain that I had
not known about Trudl's departure until after my fall;
I decided not to try.

"Tim and the little ones all send their love, and so
do my sisters. And I have brought this book, which I
had been intending to lend you; but as you are in such
poor case just now, I think you had better have it as a
gift," added Miss Sybil with her slight, fine smile. "It is

one that I used to enjoy myself very much when I was a gairl—I think it will be more suitable reading for you than Marlowe or Webster." Her glance also just brushed disapprovingly over *The Ranger*, bright pink, which Mrs. Butcher had thoughtfully laid on my bed.

"Oh, Miss Sybil, thank you—that is very kind."

"Now, my dear, as Dr. Coulthard says you should stay in bed for a couple of days, I do not think there is a great deal of point in your coming back to school anymore, since next week is the last week of term."

"So it is," I said, remembering.

I can go home, I can go with Joe, as soon as the doctor lets me up, I thought with a rush of joy.

"Miss Sybil?"

"Yes, my dear?"

"You said something once about redemption—or was it Miss Madge?"

"Redemption, child? Why do you want to know about redemption?"

"What does it mean? The word?"

"Redemption? It means to buy back or recover; or to buy somebody's freedom—a slave, for instance. Or to save or rescue."

"Like Trudl, you mean—going off to try to get her brother out of Austria?"

"Why, yes," she said, a little surprised, and added, "Your father, by the way, made a most moving speech at the International Conference on Refugees, at Évian, asking the free nations to open their doors to all the poor refugees trying to escape from Fascism."

"My father did?" I was astonished. "At Évian?"

"Yes indeed. A big conference was held there, on refugees. And he spoke, as a writer; he said it was his duty to speak for all the writers in countries where people don't have freedom to say what they think."

"Oh." I lay back weakly on my pillow. "How very—Well, I am glad he did that."

I wondered if Trudl would be glad. And if it would help her brother.

"Now, good-bye, my dear child," said Miss Sybil. "We have greatly enjoyed your brief visit." She laid her thin hand lightly on my bandaged head, gave me a brief smile, then walked out of my room. She did not mention, and I only heard long afterward, that her sister, poor Miss Lucy, who had got so drenched in yesterday's storm, contracted a severe cold which turned to pneumonia and carried her off.

Wyn called in after lunch (some thin soup made by Mrs. Butcher) and sang, "We'll all go riding on a rainbow, To a land that's far away," until I wished that I could return to my state of unconsciousness. But now I felt very wakeful; as if the sleep I had had would last me for weeks.

"Wyn," I said, in a pause, while she was peering rather disgustedly at *A Girl of the Limberlost,* the book which Miss Sybil had given me, and which I was already halfway through, "Wyn, did anyone ever find out what happened to Patty, Joshua Harkin's daughter, after he vanished?"

"Why, yes," said Wyn, surprised, "didn't I tell you? She was my great-great-great-granny."

"She was *what*?"

"Or a few more greats," Wyn allowed, "seeing it was all back in good King Charles's golden day. Anyway, she was my great-great-something granny. Because Ralph, the feller she married, *his* name was

Ralph Butcher. It's all writ down in the church regis-
ter. And Patty had a baby, called Tom, who was my
great-great-grandpa. So, see, it's all in the family. My
uncle Cyril—him that paints the pictures—he used to
tell fortunes, something amazing. Just like old Joshua.
Only he gave it up and went into the art line. He done
those ones in the museum. Mum says they look like
hens' innards. But Mr. Wood the vicar says they are
ree-markable."

"Your uncle Cyril," I said in a stunned voice,
"painted those pictures in the museum?"

"Yes, he did. Oh," hummed Wyn, "it ain't going to
rain no more, no more, It ain't a-going to rain no
more. Why in the world do the old folks say, It ain't
a-going to rain no more?"

I lay listening to her reedy voice and wondering
bemusedly about Patty's baby, about Joshua's dog,
about Cyril Butcher who was able to paint pictures of
my dreams.

"So: ain't your mum a-coming back no more?"
Wyn said inquisitively after a while.

"My stepmother? I don't know. Maybe not. My
father wants to sell this house."

"Poor old house. It'll be standing empty again,"
said Wyn sentimentally. "Nobody ever stays here
long. I told you that. Because of Joshua's curse."

"What curse?"

"He put a curse on anyone that comes here. That
they'll only lose what they value and value what they
lose. Summat like that."

But I didn't come here, I thought. I was born here.

"D'you know," Wyn went on in a tone of surprise,

"d'you know, I don't mind coming here so much as I used. It don't seem so bad now."

And presently she wandered off through the study. I could hear her voice drifting back, fainter and fainter. "Let's all sing like the birdies sing, Tweet! tweet! tweet! tweet! tweet! . . ."

MR. BELLYAP AND TIM came to see me when school was over. While Tim was kindly fetching me an apple and a glass of water, his father said, "Tim's all excited about the well in the cellar of this house. Perhaps—if the house is going to be standing empty—he and his aunt will be able to persuade the local authority to allow them to do some excavation. That, just now, is Tim's greatest wish."

"My goodness," I said faintly, thinking that Mr. Bellyap must disapprove of this, but he went on, "Do you know, I've been so glad of your company for Tim this summer. Marnie and I are always so busy. Tim's a quiet fellow, but you've got him interested in all kinds of things, new ideas, got him reading and asking questions and using his mind as you do; he'll be going off, like you, to boarding school next term, and this summer has been a real preparation for that. We were very glad," he added shyly, "to help your stepmother a bit with the fare to Paris. I do hope she is successful in getting her brother out of Austria. She has worked so very hard, learning shorthand and bookkeeping all this summer, going to evening classes at the grammar school; we have felt rather sorry for her."

Tim came back with the glass of water, and soon after that, he and his father went away; Tim and I said good-bye and promised we would write to each other, but we both knew perfectly well that such promises are never kept.

Redemption, I thought. Buying back somebody who has been a slave. Or recovering something— something that has been lost, perhaps.

Late in the afternoon my brother Joe arrived.

"Well," he said, "you are a one, aren't you? Walking in your sleep. Wild! Did you have any dreams while you were walking?"

"Oh, yes. Hundreds."

But just then I felt too sleepy to relate them. My brother Joe sat down and picked up *The Lair of the White Worm* from the heap of books on my table. He began to read and to chuckle over it.

"What terrible terrible twaddle. How can we ever have read such rubbish!"

He read on and on, thoroughly enjoying it; and in his peaceful company I went peacefully to sleep.

TWO DAYS LATER I was pronounced well enough to travel, so Joe and I caught the bus and did the journey home together. The day before I had lain on the sofa while Joe read aloud *Henry IV,* Parts I and II; which is a very funny play, specially the parts about Falstaff and Hotspur. I fell in love with Prince Hal because of the lines about him: "I saw young Harry with his beaver on, His cuisses on his thighs, gallantly armed. . . ."

When we finally arrived home, I half expected to see Joshua Harkin's black dog waiting for me, but he was not there, or not visibly. I do still sometimes feel his cold nose bump against my hand. And I dream about him at least once a week.

Trudl never came back to Harken House, and I never saw her again. I don't know if she managed to get her brother and friends out of Austria.

Tim was not granted his wish to excavate the well, for, in October, after he and I had started boarding school, Hitler invaded Czechoslovakia, and after that Poland, and then World War II began, and people were too busy to excavate cellars. The following year Dune was bombed several times. One German plane dropped a stick of firebombs before recrossing the Channel, and Harken House was burned to the ground. When the ruins were cleared away, a well was found under the cellar floor, and some bones in it, but no treasure.

My last memory of Harken House is a scene in the garden. Joe and I had gone out so that I could demonstrate my Frog airplane to him.

"This isn't really big enough, but it will have to do." My legs were still shaky.

"Let's see then," said Joe.

The little craft flew beautifully, its oiled silk sides glimmering in the clear morning light. Up and up it went, on an invisible eddy of air, which lifted and sent it soaring high over the garden wall and the next-door trees, high over the roofs of the houses in Chapel Passage, high and away over the marsh and out of sight toward the sea.

"Oh—what a pity!" said Joe. "What a shame."

But I felt queerly happy. Let it go, I thought, the airy silent thing. Let it be free. Birds sing only when they are angry or frightened, somebody told me once. Silence is best.

And yet—you know—I became a playwright too. Before I went deaf. But that was long ago.

About the Author

THE DISTINGUISHED ENGLISH WRITER Joan Aiken is the author of over fifty books for young readers and twenty-three novels for adults. Her juvenile list includes the Wolves Chronicles, featuring the intrepid Dido Twite and her friends. Her collections of creepy stories include *Give Yourself a Fright, A Touch of Chill,* and *A Whisper in the Night.*

Joan Aiken is the daughter of Conrad Aiken. She lives in Sussex, England.